To TELL You the TRUTH

To TELL You the TRUTH

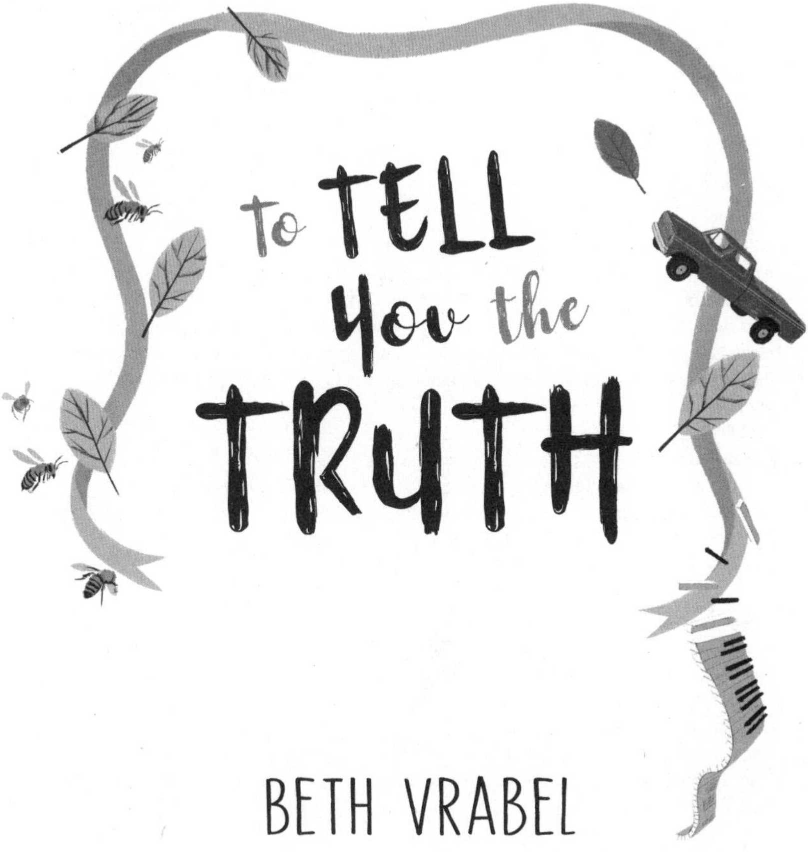

BETH VRABEL

Atheneum Books for Young Readers
New York London Toronto Sydney New Delhi

ATHENEUM BOOKS FOR YOUNG READERS
An imprint of Simon & Schuster Children's Publishing Division
1230 Avenue of the Americas, New York, New York 10020
This book is a work of fiction. Any references to historical events, real people, or real places are used fictitiously. Other names, characters, places, and events are products of the author's imagination, and any resemblance to actual events or places or persons, living or dead, is entirely coincidental.

Interior design by Irene Metaxatos
The text for this book was set in Minion Pro.
Manufactured in the United States of America
0421 FFG
First Edition
2 4 6 8 10 9 7 5 3 1
Library of Congress Cataloging-in-Publication Data
Names: Vrabel, Beth, author.
Title: To tell you the truth / Beth Vrabel.
Description: First edition. | New York : Atheneum Books for Young Readers, 2021. | Audience: Ages 8 to 12. | Summary: After her grandmother, a marvelous storyteller, dies, fourth-grader Trixy, accompanied by her friend Raymond, runs away to learn about her grandmother's mysterious past.
Identifiers: LCCN 2020029418 | ISBN 9781534478596 (hardcover) | ISBN 9781534478619 (eBook)
Subjects: CYAC: Grandmothers—Fiction. | Storytelling—Fiction.
Classification: LCC PZ7.V9838 To 2021 | DDC [Fic]—dc23
LC record available at https://lccn.loc.gov/2020029418

TO STORYTELLERS

AND ESPECIALLY STORYKEEPERS

Chapter One

Gran loves me.

This is the truth, heavy as the air this late August night. It's stronger than the throw-away thoughts that will keep my eyes open when I crawl back into bed. It's brighter than the lilacs that grow in tangles by the white stone marking Gran's eternal rest: *Dolcie B. Jacobs, beloved grandmother and mother.*

But much as she loves me, Gran hates me too.

This is the new truth that's tickling me from the inside out and twisting down, down, down to where I lock away her best stories. Including the one she told me when the sky was the blue of a newborn baby's eyes. I'll keep that one just for me, no matter what.

Because if there's one thing Gran couldn't ever stand, it's a liar. "I don't have room in this old heart for hate, Trixy," I can hear her say even now. "Except for liars and thieves."

And here's one last for-sure truth: That's just what I am. A selfish liar and a thief.

I've been lying to Mama, stealing my gran's stories, and, worst of all, I'm about to break my daddy's heart.

I'm going to run away with Raymond Crickett.

Only Raymond doesn't know it yet.

When kids at school found out that Raymond Crickett's dad was a famous musician who went on tours, everyone thought he must be super rich. Rumors put his house at three stories tall, contended that celebrities could be spotted on the rocking chairs on his porch, and that his dad did nothing but sing and strum his fiddle all the day long. People whispered that the only reason Raymond had lunch tickets for the cafeteria and patches on the knees of his jeans was that he wanted to blend in with everyone else.

But the truth was that Raymond's house was a lot like mine—only my ranch house was yellow and his was blue. We both had big front porches and tiny living rooms. Both of our dads had pushed their old trucks into the yard when the engines refused to turn the last time.

There were differences too. While Mama had planted

flowers around my house, Raymond's house had plain grass right up until the porch. The paint around the trim was flaky, and a couple of railings on the porch had splintered or broken fully off.

The house was a bit like Raymond—pleasant but not quite taken care of enough.

Raymond's dad spent a lot of time playing the fiddle, but he also had a bunch of side jobs, mostly landscaping and carpentry. Like Raymond, Mr. Crickett had big brown eyes. He also had a beard like my dad's, only Mr. Crickett's beard stretched into a point under his chin and his mustache curled up at the ends. Raymond told me once that his dad used "product" for that to happen. Tattoos ran along his arms and stretched to the sides of his neck. They were of eagles, trees, and words too swirly for me to read.

When Mr. Crickett sang, my heart paused.

Once, Mama and I went into the city and ate at a gourmet restaurant in the middle of winter. I wore a scratchy dress with silver ruffles and Mama had her hair twisted into a bun atop her head like a ballerina. Snow fell outside the windows, and all around us people rushed and slid on sidewalks. Inside the café, it was warm enough to fog the windows. Mama nibbled on a layered cookie that had cost seven dollars. I ordered a hot chocolate, and it arrived in a gold-rimmed red mug with a huge pile of twisting whipped cream on top. I remembered that first sip, how it seemed to pour straight down to the tips of my toes, filling me with sweetness, making every silly thing I had worried about—what the other diners thought of me, whether I was wearing the right dress or saying the right things—melt away.

Mr. Crickett's voice was like that first sip of cocoa. I couldn't be scared when he sang.

But unfortunately, he wasn't singing when I crept down the street to their house in the dark of night.

I was sure I was about to be in a world of trouble. Mr. Crickett was loading the bed of the truck with bags and equipment while talking into a cell phone tucked in the crook of his neck. Sara, Raymond's sister, leaned against the passenger side, scowling at him. I sneaked past them, moving silent as could be, toward the house.

I found Raymond sitting on the front porch stoop. He jumped when he saw me pop up beside the railing. "Trixy, what are you doing here?" he gasped.

I whispered, "I *told* you I was coming along with you on your daddy's tour, didn't I?"

"You most certainly did not." Raymond's head swiveled from side to side, making sure no one saw us. "You said you *wanted* to come along. That's different. And *then* today you assaulted Catrina and got kicked out of school!" he said. "Dad saw a bunch of police cars and an ambulance going to your house too! What happened to you? I thought maybe you done lost your mind! You been saying such wild things lately!"

I scrunched my face and crossed my arms. "Raymond Crickett, my mind is right where I left it inside my head. Now's the time to use yours. How can I get into your truck without your dad or sister seeing me?"

Chapter Two

The first time I thought about running away was three weeks earlier. I came down to breakfast, making myself look as pathetic as possible with a sloppy ponytail and droopy face, hoping to convince Mama once again that I was too forlorn for school. I planned to tell her I was sick, which wasn't a total lie. Already my stomach was churning, churning, churning, just about at the nonstop boiling it had kept up all through school this year.

But instead, I saw a note next to a plate of sliced apples topped with peanut butter. *See you after school. Daddy's upstairs if you need anything.*

I looked out the window, spotting Mama running up the street. Running? What was happening to our family?

Daddy had worked the third shift the night before, so he was out cold upstairs with the fan blasting in his face. Mama was getting farther and farther away from me. I could get up from the table and head off to see all the places I knew about but had never seen. Places like Memphis, where the music comes from every corner, draping like a blanket of sound to tuck in the town. Places like Nevada, where the desert fries you like an egg in a buttered pan until the sun sinks and makes your breath turn to frosty clouds, all in the same day. Places like Montana, where the sky is wider and thicker than the ground, and standing there under all that sky makes things such as mud boiling right in its pocket of ground seem almost all right. Places like the loft of a dusty Tennessee barn, where a girl could fling herself into thin air and be cradled by hay that somehow loses its tendency to scratch when it's called upon to save your life.

Thanks to Gran, I knew about all these places, though I've only ever seen but one place myself.

But I just walked down the dirt driveway to stand by the mailbox, where the school bus would pick me up.

The doors to the bus opened, parting the air, and for just a second I thought I smelled that bubbling Montana mud Gran had told me about while boiling eggs for salad last summer. But as soon as the doors creaked closed behind me, all I smelled was stinky Raymond Crickett. Okay, maybe it was the school bus itself that smelled that way, but my nose wrinkled just the same.

The only other person on the bus was Sara, Raymond's sister. She sat in the last row, her knees folded with her head resting on them so all I saw was the top of her hair, which she had dyed turquoise over the summer. Most high schoolers drove themselves to school, but Sara's eyes worked differently, and she used the bus. The high school was the last stop, and Sara usually slept through most of the pickups and drop-offs.

No such luck with Raymond. His eyes worked just fine and he never napped. He perched in the middle seat of the bus and, just like those shuddery pictures of the dead and buried, his eyes followed me no matter where I sat on that stinking bus.

If I was in the front row, right behind the driver, Raymond Crickett's eyes—his whole body, really—tilted my way. If I sat in the way back, same thing. He was so much everywhere on that bus that the only way to feel like any space was my own was to plunk down in the seat right beside him. That way he had to twist to see me and I knew for a fact it was no accident.

To think, he used to be my best friend.

"I wasn't sure you'd be on the bus 'gain today, Trixy,"

Raymond said. I shuddered as the driver shifted gears. Raymond's eyes got all watery.

I was about to tell him to mind his own beeswax, and just because *I* didn't want to ride the bus, didn't want to be in any sort of car, that didn't mean *he* could get all teary eyed about it. But then the driver stopped the bus, opened the door, and let in the next group of kids. With them came the softest breeze, smelling like lilacs, and suddenly all I could see was Gran. She wouldn't like those unfriendly words hurled at anyone, especially Raymond.

"So, what'd you write about for the memoir?" Raymond asked, making the last word sound like "memo-or."

I didn't need to ask Raymond what he wrote about. I knew it was about his dad, and his upcoming tour across the South with a string band called the Crickett Quintet. When Raymond and I were in first grade, Mr. Crickett was just a guy with a lot of tattoos and a fiddle hanging on the wall of the living room. Then Raymond's mom left them, taking the dog with her but leaving Sara and Raymond. Mr. Crickett started plucking away at the strings of that fiddle. Gran and I used to go for long walks that wound up going past their house almost every night. Sometimes we'd be on their porch, singing along to Mr. Crickett's songs. After a long while, Raymond and Sara would sing too.

Wouldn't you know it? Gran started talking about

places in Tennessee where she had heard bluegrass music just like his. And soon enough, Mr. Crickett not only had a real band, he had a list of places that wanted him to come and play, written out and handed over by Gran. She had a knack for things like that—plotting the next chapter in people's stories and helping them turn the page. Months earlier, before the accident, she told us she wanted to go along on the next Tennessee tour with Mr. Crickett's band, and that she wanted to take me too.

The bus lurched forward with a *squelch*, or maybe that was just the sound of all my guts liquifying into sudden panic stew. "It's okay," Raymond said. His arm shot out to keep me in place. "We're okay."

"I'm not worried about the bus," I snapped. Okay, I lied. Again. I don't like being in cars or buses much. Raymond dropped his arm. "I'm worried about that stupid assignment," I said. "I sort of forgot to do it." Sort of like how I forgot to do all my homework, classwork too, if I was being honest, these first three weeks of school.

The bus rumbled to a stop in front of Clarkville Primary School and my soon-to-be fourth-grade doom. Right on cue, my stomach reached a boil.

Chapter Three

By accident I overheard Mrs. Brown talking to my parents that afternoon when I was supposed to be thinking about my choices in the hallway. I knew it was going to happen, that sometime soon Mrs. Brown would on-purpose ruin my life. But I didn't think one simple mistake—not turning in the memoir—would mean she'd pick up the phone and call in my parents *that day*. I mean, I offered to *tell* her my life's story, but she just rolled her eyes and shook her head all at once. (That takes skill, by the way. I've tried it in front of the mirror. Even braided my hair in a thick rope like Mrs. Brown's and put on a turtleneck like she always wore, to pull the picture together. But I couldn't do it. Or maybe I did but couldn't see it since I was, you know, rolling my eyes and shaking my head.)

The thing is, they were talking on the far side of the room by Mrs. Brown's desk. I guess she thought that'd be enough distance so their voices wouldn't seep out from under the thin door and up through my toes to settle in my ears. And maybe she would've been right, had it been any other parents than mine. But Daddy's ears were ringing since it had been blasting week at the quarry. Mrs. Brown kept having to talk louder and louder, and Daddy kept saying, "What? What'd you say, now?" which led Mama to repeating what Mrs. Brown said louder still until I think even Raymond Crickett could've heard it from the bus ride home.

"She's a storyteller!" Mrs. Brown shouted.

"A what?" Daddy answered, right over Mama screeching, "She makes up stories!"

"Stories?" Daddy said back.

"Yes!" Mama and Mrs. Brown agreed.

"What?"

"She makes them up!"

At this, Daddy chuckled. "'Course she does. Gets it natural."

This time, Mrs. Brown was the one who said, "What?"

"Trixy gets storytelling natural," Daddy boomed. "Her

gran, Jenny's mama, she would whisper story after story in Trixy's ear from the time she was a baby until she passed."

"I'm sorry." Mrs. Brown's voice had dipped down into that dying-is-sad-so-we-whisper tone. I leaned forward in my chair to hear.

Mama cleared her throat. "Yes, well, she was nearly forty when she had me; she reached her eighties, so her life was long."

Something twisted inside me. Mama said this to everyone who seemed sad about Gran. While sure Gran had been old enough for the tops of her hands to have tea-colored stains, for creases around her eyes, for afternoon naps, she was *young* as me too. We'd played in the creek, splashing each other until our clothes stuck like skin, just three days before it happened. She was young enough to laugh when a butterfly landed on her nose, and young enough to eat cookie batter from the spoon, young enough to dance with me on the living room rug, young enough to look up at the stars and still have wishes.

She was young enough to live a lot longer.

"When did she die?" Mrs. Brown asked.

Mama, I guessed, was tired of that tone too, since when she answered she did so loud and firm. "About six months back. In the middle of third grade."

I scooted back in my chair, wishing the door were

thicker after all. After the accident, all the doctors had told Daddy and Mama that I was fine, that my seat belt kept me safe and only the outside of my chest had been bruised. But they were wrong, because a sharp pebble got wedged behind my ribs. I felt it all the time, even though Daddy told me again and again that it wasn't real, that they would've seen it on the X-rays. He called it grief, but it was a rock. And when Mama talked like this, like Gran's dying was just something that had happened in the past, that rock poked my ribs, so sharp that my heart pounded and my palms sweat and my chest hurt.

"Hmm," Mrs. Brown said, her voice back to normal now too. "That could explain some of Trixy's difficulties. Grief makes us do odd things."

"Difficulties? What are the difficulties with storytelling? Don't you want kids to write and read stories?" Mama asked.

"All she does is talk!" Mrs. Brown said.

"What?" This time Mama and Daddy said it together.

"All she does is talk!" Mrs. Brown bellowed. "During my lessons, during quiet reading time, during gym class, during lunch. Talk, talk, talk, talk! I can't take it!" Mrs. Brown sucked in her breath so loud, I could hear it. When she spoke next, her tone was hard but not as high. "For such a tiny thing, she has a loud voice."

I glanced down at myself. So what if I was the shortest, skinniest fourth grader that Nurse Bev had ever seen? (She always laughed at the number on the scale when I went in for my yearly checkup. Told Mama, "She was born no bigger than a bean. Might make it to sprout size before she's grown." Mama always fretted—"I make her drink milk! Eat vegetables!"—but Nurse Bev said not to worry, that I'm growing as I should for someone who started out bean sized. Someday I'll remind her that we all started out bean sized. Besides, I was born weighing four pounds, and four-pound babies are more like cantaloupes than beans.)

That didn't mean I didn't have big, loud stories.

"Trixy's so busy talking that she doesn't do her work! I have yet to see her get through a single exam, let alone turn in homework!"

"You don't assign homework! Trixy never has any." Mama slapped Daddy's arm. She does that when she gets worked up sometimes.

"I give out homework every night!"

"Every night?" Daddy repeated. He didn't need Mrs. Brown to speak any louder. She was plain yelling, louder now than that time Raymond Crickett got the pencil stuck up his nose. (He sneezed, and it flew across the room. I laughed so hard.)

"Didn't you get any of my notes?" Mrs. Brown said.

"Notes?"

Oh, I was in a worse situation than that poor pencil now. Suddenly fear nipped at my armpits like fire ants.

All three of them got quiet. Too quiet.

"Trixy!" Mrs. Brown shouted. I heard the creak of her chair pushing back as she stood. Soon she was beside me. She gestured for me to follow her. "Come on in here. I think we could use some explanations from you."

And wouldn't you know it? For the first time ever in her classroom, I didn't have a thing to say, but that old Mrs. Brown was still upset.

"Well, Trixy," Mama prodded. "We need an explanation. What's wrong?"

I shrugged, eyes fixed on my shoelaces. One was just a smidgen too long. It dragged under my shoe when I walked and made me wobbly. But I knew Mama, Daddy, and Mrs. Brown didn't want to talk about my shoelace issues just then.

Besides, how could I explain what had come over me this year? I couldn't understand it myself. All I knew was that once Gran moved from her bedroom off the kitchen to rest in the ground under that lilac bush, all the words that had ever been clogged up inside me gurgled to the surface like those geysers in Yellowstone. Mine only seemed to erupt when I was at school.

I opened my mouth to try and say something, but then I saw Mama's pinched-up face. Just like always, she was holding in her own geyser, one of grief, and all my words disappeared again. Why was it that the more Mama kept inside, the more I felt like I would explode?

Mama patted my hand. "When you was a baby bean," she started, and internally I corrected her—I even glanced up at Mrs. Brown and saw she too was mouthing *were* instead of *was*, "you cried all day long. All night long, even. We didn't know what to do with you. You just had so much to say. So, so much." Mama smiled at Daddy. "Remember that?"

"What?" Daddy yanked on his ears, trying to get them to pop. I looked at him and yawned widely. He did too, since yawns are contagious. His eyes widened and he grinned when his ears finally popped. "That's better," he said in his regular voice. "Now what was that, Jenny?"

Mama swatted his arm again. "I said, remember how Trixy used to cry, back when she was a baby?"

Daddy nodded and leaned back, crossing his arms and his long legs. "'Course I do. No one could quiet her. All red-faced fury and screaming like a beet would 'bout being yanked from the ground." His chuckle faded a little when he spoke next. "Until your mama figured out the trick, Jenny."

Mama's face pinched up again. She stiffened a bit and turned back toward Mrs. Brown.

"What was the trick?" Mrs. Brown asked like Daddy was about to give her a plate full of cotton candy.

"Dolcie's stories. Story after story after story, right into her little ear. Trixy would go still and blink like an owl, like she could just picture whatever nonsense her gran was harvesting."

"It wasn't nonsense!" I blurted. "All of 'em were true!"

Mama swatted Daddy's arm again. "I've heard snippets of those stories all my life. Stories about grand adventures that weren't possible for that woman. Stories about her family, though she never had any. No one believed her tall tales."

"They were true." I stomped my foot. But since I was sitting, it didn't really have much of an impact. "I believe them."

"What happened?" Mrs. Brown asked gently. "Cancer?"

Mama shook her head. "Car accident. Trixy was in the backseat."

No one spoke. All my words evaporated in a *poof*. Everything *poofed*—Mama, Daddy, Mrs. Brown, the classroom. Gone, gone, gone. For a second, all I saw was a swirl of colors and the sound of a scream. I didn't know if it was mine or Gran's, but I hoped it was mine. I rubbed my knuckles over the rock in my ribs. Mama patted my arm, bringing me back to the classroom.

"None of us, I'm guessing, have been the same since." Daddy sat up straight again, with a sideways glance at Mama, who for sure wasn't the same. Not now that she was running, eating mostly salads or nothing at all, and wasn't nearly as cushiony to hug.

After a moment of the four of us all looking down at our own shoelaces, Mrs. Brown cleared her throat. "As I said, grief can make us do unusual things. I'm willing to move past these first three weeks of school. Start fresh tomorrow."

"That's real kind of you," Mama said.

Mrs. Brown and I silently mouthed *really*.

"On one condition," Mrs. Brown said, and thus launched right back into dooming my entire life.

I stared at the glowing ghost-face of a blank document page on the computer. This was the second time I thought about running away, though I didn't have a plan yet and I certainly wasn't thinking of Raymond Crickett.

"All you got to do is fill it up with words, Trixy," said Mama, her hand on my shoulder as I sat at the desk. "All those words that cram inside you and burst through at school. Let them out here."

I shook my head.

"All Mrs. Brown wants is a three-page story every week. It don't have to be good. Just a story."

I held my fingers over the keyboard. "She wants this one to be a memoir, about something true that happened."

Mama squeezed my shoulder. "I can think of something you might want to talk about."

"I can't talk about Gran," I said, facing the blank screen so I wouldn't see the hurt on Mama's face at using the name. "Gran always told me her stories were just for me. So I can't share them." *Remember, Trixy, stories aren't the same if the wrong person hears them. They don't settle in their ears right. That's why my stories are just for you and only you.*

Mama didn't say anything for so long that I thought she had left the room. But then she whispered, "She's gone. None of that matters anymore."

I wanted to argue with Mama, tell her that Gran still was here, that I felt her all the time. But she wouldn't believe me any more than she'd believe the adventures Gran had. I propped my feet onto the chair, rested my arms around my knees, and let my head drop. I peeked out the window. The stars were bragging about not having to do any schoolwork as they floated in space. Mama patted me one more time and left to go exercise to a fitness video in the basement. Maybe I should be more like Mama; get in line and move on.

Gran used to stare at the stars at night. I didn't want to, but I remembered.

"What are you doing?" I had asked Gran as she looked up at the brightest star in the sky.

"Oh, nothing," Gran had said, a smile tugging at her cheeks. "Just telling her I love her."

"The star?" I laughed, and Gran tickled the spot between my shoulders, singing a song about wishing upon a star as she did it.

"Gran, can you write down that story you just told me?" I had asked her. Even though all the stories she told me were about her and her sister, she told them like they had happened to someone else. She even used their childhood nicknames: Dollie and Lil Sis.

"Write it down? Now, why would I do that?" And even though I was just remembering, my ears tingled and I heard her voice same as if she was whispering straight into them all over again. She has the best voice—*had* the best voice. That last, thick, honey-soaked sip of tea that makes slugging down the whole cup of hot, bittery water worthwhile.

"So I can read it over and over again. So I can show it to my friends!"

Gran laughed as though I had told her I was in love with Raymond Crickett. "No one believes my stories but you, Trixy Mae. And they're just for you. If I wrote them down, they'd be picked apart. When I only tell them to you, they're free, like you and me." Gran had twirled, making her long dress swirl around to tickle my legs from where I sat at her feet.

"But if they're all true like you say," I had whispered, "everyone would have to believe them. Because true is true is true. That's what Mama says."

She had tugged on my earlobe and chuckled. "My stories will land the right way in your ears alone. Love does that, you know. It's the only magic there is. It makes you hear each other in just the way you should be heard."

Remembering that now, my heart hammered. I stopped the memory in its place, popping out of my seat and moving to the window before it could continue another second.

The night was clear and dark. If I stood on my tiptoes, I could see the lilac bushes surrounded by the white picket fence at the far edge of our yard. But I didn't do that tonight. I looked at the stars. One was much brighter than the others. Closing my eyes, I tried to make a wish, but it came out as an apology instead.

Gran, I'm sorry. But I don't have any stories of my own.

The next morning, I got on the bus and sat in the front row.

When the driver stopped, Raymond Crickett moved

from the middle to sit with me, plopping down on the bench seat so hard all the air huffed out like a fart. “What’s wrong with you today?”

“Nothing,” I said.

“Something’s wrong,” he said. “Are you worked up because of me?”

I forgot my promise to not talk so much and turned to Raymond. “Now, why would I be upset ’bout you?”

Raymond’s cheeks flushed a deep red. “Well, ’cause we’ve been making so many plans for the road trip and you were going to come with us, but now . . .”

I crossed my arms and faced the back of the driver’s bald head. “I happen to have been busy, Raymond. Too busy to think about your stupid road trip.”

Raymond didn’t say anything for a long time. “It’s not stupid, Trixy.”

I didn’t answer.

In the classroom, I took my seat at the desk in the back and tried to make myself as small and quiet as possible, keeping my words bottled inside. They pushed against my lips, threatening to explode. My hands twisted the story I’d printed out. I knew Gran wouldn’t like that I was sharing one of her stories, and I for sure knew typing it in straight lines would be even worse.

"What's wrong with you? You sick?" asked Miranda Sherman, who had the misfortune of sitting next to me. And of being a hair sucker. The last inch of her thick brown hair always was soggy. But thanks to the talk geyser inside me, this was the first time she had had an opportunity to speak.

I shook my head, not trusting myself to open my mouth.

Despite how small I had made myself, Mrs. Brown found me and stood next to my desk. Her scent, a mixture of baby powder, pencil shavings, and righteous judgment, swirled around me. "Well, Trixy, we're only a few minutes into class, but I can see already that you're more composed! Did you write the story, as I asked?"

I paused, then nodded. Mrs. Brown put out her hand.

I didn't move.

"May I *have* your memoir, please?"

I nodded again.

Mrs. Brown sighed and crossed her arms. "Really, Trixy? Why must you make everything so difficult?"

I copied her sigh and smoothed the pages where my fingers had worried the corners. Then I handed them to Mrs. Brown.

"Wow," she murmured. "I only asked for three pages."

A little flicker in my chest was proud that the story

ended up being six pages. It swirled around inside with all the other about-to-burst feelings that pushed against me from the inside out.

"You know, you can speak. I like that you talk. I just don't want you to talk *all the time*." Mrs. Brown looked at me.

"Okay," I whispered.

"Okay." Mrs. Brown finally turned to go back to the front of the class. "Oh, wait!" She slapped the pages onto the desk. "You forgot to put your name at the top. How else will I know whose story this is?"

I pulled a pencil out from my desk and wrote *Trixy Mae Williams* across the top, my ears ringing so hard I guess I knew what Daddy felt like on blasting day. This made it official. I was truly stealing one of Gran's only-for-me stories and handing it to Mrs. Brown as though it were mine to give.

"Trixy," Mrs. Brown said in her what-have-I-done-to-deserve-this-child voice, "why are you pulling such faces?"

I bit my lip before I could blurt out another not-mine story.

Mrs. Brown shook her head. "Are you feeling well, Trixy?"

I shook my head, turned it into a nod, and rubbed at my ringing ears.

She sighed again, then tucked the story under her arm, walking away.

"No matter," Miranda Sherman said. "Lots of kids get ear infections." Her father was the pediatrician in town and so she always behaved as though she knew everything there was to know about healing. "My daddy will fix you up."

"What?" I said before remembering I was clamping down on words.

"Your ears," she said. "You keep rubbing them."

I sat on my hands.

Miranda narrowed her eyes. "What was your story about, anyway?"

"Dollie and Lil Sis."

"You wrote about a doll? *Ha!*" Miranda threw back her head, slobbery hair sticking to her cheeks.

"I did *not*," I told her over the buzzing in my ears. "I told a story about *Dollie* and *her* little sister. That was my gran's name when she was a girl—Dollie."

"Sounds boring," Miranda said, then licked out for another strand.

"You're boring."

"Trixy!" Miranda gasped.

Next to me, Raymond chuckled. "Gran was a lot of things, but she was never boring."

I put my head down on my arms, not wanting to talk about Gran with anyone, especially Raymond Crickett. Gran *had* been a lot of things, but after stealing her story like that, I took some comfort that once upon a time, she also had been a thief, just like me.

Chapter Four

Here's the story I stole from Gran.

ONCE UPON A TIME, back when everyone called Gran Dollie, she resembled me—small and stick skinny, long curly hair, and eyes too big for her triangle face. Only my eyes are dark as night, while Dollie's were the same then as when I last saw them, a sky so blue that for a moment you forget to breathe.

For three years, longer than they'd ever stayed anywhere, Dollie and Lil Sis lived near a bakery in Sweetheart Mountain, a little town near Jackson, Tennessee.

Dollie gazed through the bakery window, ballooning up her lungs with sugar-sweet air. A sign on the door proclaimed NO UNACCOMPANIED CHILDREN ALLOWED. "Breathe deep," she said to Lil Sis. "We'll fool our bellies."

But Lil Sis's bottom lip puckered. "My belly's too smart for that." Whereas Dollie was smoke-black hair and cloud-white skin, Lil Sis was sun-lit hair and suntanned skin. Dollie could imagine that pastry melting on her tongue; Lil Sis only felt her hollow belly.

The bakery was owned by a couple as tough as day-old bread. In voices gruff as sandpaper, they'd call to each other. "Dear, I need more flour." Or "Darling, we're low on cinnamon." Always, the old man was called Dear. Always the old woman, Darling. Alongside them was their daughter, who lived with them, and her small son. Dear and Darling simply called her Honey.

And, wouldn't you know it, that baby thought his mama's name was Honey too! Baby must've escaped his babysitter, because he tapped the back window of the bakery, calling out, "Honey, let me hold you!"

"Now, Baby," Honey called back, "you know you aren't allowed in here! It isn't safe."

When Baby cried, Lil Sis whimpered alongside him. "It's too much to handle. They have all that happy locked up in that bakery. And they keep it all to themselves. It ain't right."

The girls were short on happy, that was for sure. That morning, Mother and Father had pushed the sisters onto the front porch and locked the door. They talked in loud voices, back and forth. "What are they doing?" Lil Sis had asked Dollie.

"Telling each other stories we aren't able to hear yet."

When they opened the door again, both smiled with their teeth trapping secrets.

They left again that afternoon, telling the girls to be ready to hit the road when they returned the next day. This happened sometimes, especially to girls whose parents said they lived where the wind took them. Even if small girls felt roots reach from their bare feet into the soil they ran across, even if they dreamed of someday rolling out dough in a kitchen with steamed-up windows.

Now, peering inside the warm bakery, Dollie turned to Lil Sis. "We're going to go in. First chance we get, sign or no sign. We're going in."

Just as I had when I first heard this story, I held my breath while writing this part. Maybe Gran and I were alike in lots of ways—from the tiny freckle we both had on our palm to our love of square dancing—but we sure were different too. Here Dollie is about to be on-purpose bad, about to surely get in heaps of trouble. Before I stole this story from Gran, about the closest I ever got to doing something so clear-as-day wrong was when I fibbed about having my eyes all the way shut during rounds of Heads Up, Seven Up.

But then again, maybe we don't know we're capable of doing something until a situation presents itself. After all, I didn't know it yet, sitting there in my room writing this story, but in just a couple of weeks, I'd hurt everyone I loved to run away with Raymond Crickett.

The first chance Dollie and Lil Sis got to break into Sweetheart Bakery came moments later. Something was *different* in the bakery that day. Every once in a while, Darling would curl her hands under her chin like a little girl and say, "Can you believe it, Dear? Can you believe this is happening?"

"What's going on?" Lil Sis whispered.

Dollie shook her head. She bent low and peered across the bakery to the back window for Baby's face. There it was, nicely framed, him watching her. He waved with three little fingers.

All the happy and sweet stayed right in the bakery as Dear popped his head out the door. "You two, scat now. We've got to concentrate. It's a big day. Big!" And with that Dear slammed shut the door. Dollie gasped, at war with herself. On one hand was the absolute that when a grown-up tells you to do something, you must.

On the other hand? She would have one of those sweet treats. She *would*.

Dollie turned to form a plan with Lil Sis, but she was nowhere to be found. Peeking once more through the glass wall of the bakery, she spotted Lil Sis's face alongside Baby's in the back window, both of them staring hungrily into the bakery. Dollie darted around to the back of the building just in time to see the most marvelous sight.

A piano made entirely of cake.

The icing was black as night. The keys glimmered like real ivory. All three of them sucked in their breath.

At that moment, the bakery's front doorbell rang out. A flurry of people rushed in, each of them in a thick fur coat and hat, despite the warm southern winter. In the middle of them all was a magnificent man, his dark hair swirled into a cloud atop his head, his face smooth, with pink, shining lips and a dimple in the middle of his chin. His white shirt was trimmed in lace along the edges of his sleeves and collar. He wore a tight-fitting black jacket with a dark lace overlay. A bright red sash cinched his narrow waist. Even his shoes were fancy—covered with swirls of shiny leather.

Dear rushed forward. "Sir, thank you so much for being here today!" He shook the man's heavily ringed hand.

Darling wiped her hands again and again on her apron. Honey smoothed her hair and smiled wide.

"This is our moment," Dollie breathed, and whispered a plan flimsy as spun sugar.

Baby was first up. He tapped on the window. "Let me hold you, Honey!" he cried.

Inside, Darling held the piano-shaped cake in her thick arms as Dear proudly pointed out the specially designed keys and lettering. Honey glanced up at the window, shaking her head at Baby. He rapped the window with his knuckles. "Honey! Let me *hold you*!"

The piano player and fur-draped women turned

toward the window. Darling and Dear turned along with them. The huge piano cake wobbled in Darling's arms.

"*Now!*" Dollie whispered.

Lil Sis threw open the back door, dashing between the fancy man's legs through the bakery toward the door in the front. Dear bellowed, "*Stop!*" Arms waving, he rushed toward her.

Darling turned, holding the cake. Honey covered her mouth with her hands.

Again, Baby rapped on the window, but this time, he shouted, "Run! Run! *Run!*"

Dollie slipped into the bakery. Her hands darted out again and again to the display cases lining the front window. She nabbed beignets, croissants, cakes, and sugared buns, and pushed them down the front of her dress before the door cinched shut. Her hand was closing around the treat that had starred in her dreams—the circle of flaky pastry with a dollop of sweet cream in the center—when she felt the prickly sensation of a set of eyes upon her.

Looking up, Dollie locked gazes with the fancy piano man. His thick black eyebrows were raised like two flying geese. Slowly—or maybe it was just the way Dollie's heart forgot to beat that made the moment pause—the man's left eyelid lowered in a wink.

Dollie didn't have more room for the danish inside her dress, so she shoved it into her mouth. The piano man's head tipped back as he silently laughed. As he turned, Dollie saw that the back of his jacket had the image of a piano stitched into it.

Dollie headed for the front door as Baby's bellowing shifted to, "Stop! Stop! Stop!" Lil Sis, her face split with a grin and hands full of cake and cookies, sprinted toward her.

The giant, glistening cake in Darling's arms wobbled as Dear tromped after Lil Sis. His foot hit a glob of splattered icing and he teetered. His arms windmilled to the sides, whipping Darling. Her arms wiggled, wobbled, and *whoosh!*

The cake flew into the air.

Baby pounded the glass with his little fists. Dollie scurried to hold open the front door, Lil Sis sliding out like a baseball player coming home. And the cake! Oh, the cake!

That beautiful piano cake hovered in the air as though by the sheer will of everyone in the room. And then . . . *wham!*

Splat! Right over Dear, Darling, and Honey. Right over the ladies in the fur jackets. Right over the fanciest man Dollie had ever seen. All of them screamed—except for the piano man. He stood with his arms outstretched, as though conducting an orchestra. Cake plopped over them all, especially him.

When it settled, although she knew she should run, Dollie had to look back.

The piano man licked the corners of his mouth, taking in the rich, dark cake, and threw back his head as he laughed. "Oh, now," he said, and flicked icing and cake off his heavily ringed hands. "I do so love spectacular adornments, but this truly takes the cake!"

A light flashed as one of the people accompanying the fancy piano player took a photograph.

The man winked at the photographer, and then pulled a jewel-encrusted wallet from the inside of his jacket. "We'll take it all," the man said, "everything in the shop." Then he turned toward the door and beckoned the girls back inside.

He sat down right in the middle of the cake-covered shop. Brave as could be, Dollie sat beside him, sharing a danish with him as Lil Sis licked handfuls of icing from her fingers, as Baby reached to be held by Honey, and Dear and Darling filled trays with sweet treats for all to sample.

Chapter Five

At recess, some sixth-grade boys surrounded Raymond Crickett. "No way could *your* dad be famous. You've got to be adopted," one boy said. He laughed like a donkey.

Raymond's face got splotchy. "I never said he was famous. But people pay money to listen to him play. He's real good."

Donkey Boy laughed again. "Prove it. Sing just like him, Raymond."

The other boys chanted. "Sing! Sing! Sing!"

Raymond's whole face got so red it looked about to erupt like a science fair volcano. His mouth flopped open and shut. "Leave him alone," I shouted. Raymond blinked, as surprised as me by the outburst. "His daddy *is* famous! He goes on world tours and everything."

"Well, not really the world. Just across Tennessee," Raymond muttered.

"Huh, huh, huh," Donkey Boy brayed. "Sure, I bet he brings you both on stage too."

"Why do you have to be so ugly?" I said to the boy. "Leave us alone."

The boy snorted. "Getting your girlfriend to fight for you, loser?"

"Oh, you shut your—"

That moment, Mrs. Brown leaned out of the recess doors, calling my name and sending Donkey Boy and his friends running.

"I wish you *were* coming with me on the tour," Raymond whispered. And then he wiped at his splotchy cheeks, making that rock in my chest wobble and poke at my ribs. "I wish you and Gran both were."

"Yeah, well," I snapped at him as Mrs. Brown called me again. "Get in line."

Now Mrs. Brown sat in front of me at my desk, her eyes piercing mine and her chin taking refuge in her short-sleeved turtleneck sweater. Outside, the late August air was a steaming wet quilt straight from the washing machine, but Mrs. Brown's air-conditioned classroom was crisp and cool. Having just come inside, I was caught between sweat and shiver.

"The assignment, Trixy, was to write a true story from your life."

I nodded.

"Was what you submitted a *true story*?"

I nodded again.

"From *your life*?"

I nodded a third time.

Mrs. Brown clasped her hands in front of her. "Did you actually write that story, Trixy Mae Williams?"

Once more, I nodded.

Mrs. Brown blinked at me. I blinked back.

"Trixy, Liberace died in 1987."

I tilted my head, trying to puzzle out this conversational turn. "That's interesting, ma'am."

"*You* hadn't been born yet when he died."

"Yes, Mrs. Brown."

Her cheeks pinked. Her chin escaped its hold. Her hands flexed. "How then could you *possibly* have dumped a cake on top of Liberace?"

I clasped my hands the way she held hers, trying to establish some sort of order to this bizarre conversation. "I'm not sure who Liberace is, Mrs. Brown, but my gran told me that story, and it's true as sugar is sweet."

Mrs. Brown pressed her lips together so hard the blood couldn't get to the edges, making a white line around her mouth. Her eyes drifted and she drummed her fingers along the top of the table. *Drumming* isn't quite the right word; more like her fingers tapped.

Her chin jutted upward. A shocking thing happened in that moment—I realized Mrs. Brown had once been a little girl.

A little girl maybe even a lot like me. My ears buzzed with the thought.

That buzzing became words, Mrs. Brown's story, even though her mouth didn't open. Somehow, I heard that story trickling right into my ears. It was from when Mrs. Brown was a little girl, maybe even younger than me, pretending her plain oak dresser was a shiny black baby grand piano, her fingers flying across the top.

I pressed my hands over my tingling ears and looked at the real Mrs. Brown. Her eyes focused on something over my head, something very far away, a faint smile on her face.

"I didn't know you played the piano," I said.

Mrs. Brown's smile shook and that little girl inside *poofed* into the air. "I didn't. I don't. We never had music lessons in our house or in my school. I never . . ." She straightened her fingers and lay them flat on the table.

"Well, now." Mrs. Brown pulled in a big breath and tucked her chin again. "You wrote a lovely story. Maybe not quite *your* memoir and certainly not based in fact, but nevertheless lovely."

"No!" I blurted. "It *is* true. Gran said it was."

Mrs. Brown watched me steadily, even as the bell pierced through the school. "I liked your story. You're a gifted storyteller; as your dad said, you seem to get the trait naturally. I will count this as credit toward your missing work. *However* . . ."

My breath shot out at that heavy *however*, which was sure to further ruin my life.

Mrs. Brown peered down at me. "The next story you write for me better be *true*."

Our porch swing was an old pew from the church where Mama and Daddy got married. When the church was remodeled, Daddy brought home the pew on the back of his truck. He cut off the legs and turned it into a swing, which he hung to face toward the road.

I sat there, letting my toes push me back and forth while I contemplated my life.

I didn't have one good story.

I blamed Mama and Daddy. Couldn't they have abandoned me overnight in bear-infested woods just once?

Locked me in a dark cupboard under the stairs or left me to sleep on the cold floor with only the ashes of the fireplace to warm my bones? All of this decent parenting kept me from feeling the proper amount of strife necessary to have a compelling story.

As I sat there, I counted how many times Mama ran down the stretch of road that winds around our house. She got to the mailbox, turned around, went past our house to the farmhouse behind us, around their donkey field, and back to the mailbox. All the while, a cloud of kicked-up dirt chased her. When she flipped around at the mailbox, she ran right through that cloud, scattering it away.

Twenty-two times so far.

“Mama!” I called. “Can you help me with my homework?”

“Not now, Trixy,” she puffed. “Maybe in a little.” Mama used to sit beside me while I finished my assignments every night. But ever since Gran . . . Mama didn’t do anything like she used to do. Sometimes a wicked part of me felt like both of them had been in the car that night, and Mama had turned into a ghost.

The screen door creaked as Daddy stepped onto the porch. With the sun coming down behind him, his usually brown hair was penny red. He rubbed at his scruffy beard and then settled beside me, making the pew dip down with his weight. I slid toward him a little.

We watched Mama running back and forth.

"Daddy, do you think Gran ever shared a danish with Liberace?"

Daddy yawned. "Liberace? The music man?" He rustled his bristles with his knuckles. "I sincerely doubt it, Trixy. She and he wouldn't be in the same circles, so to speak. Gran's life wasn't easy, from what I've gathered. Most of it was downright dark." His eyes followed the cloud that trailed Mama as she ran toward the sunset. "Maybe she told herself stories to get by. Maybe she passed them on to you."

Daddy's chest inflated like a balloon as he breathed in. His heavy arm wrapped around my shoulder and pulled me closer as he let all that hot air out over us both. Snug with my cheek on his chest, I could hear the *thump, thump* of his heart. It matched Mama's steps as she ran.

"Could've been true," I said. "She could've shared sweets with Liberace."

Thump, thump, thump. Run, run, run.

"Best to let some stories go," Daddy murmured as Mama passed through another cloud. Maybe that's why Mama ran so much. Maybe she was trying to shake loose her own stories.

But it felt like she was running from me.

The breeze coming through my bedroom window smelled like summer as I sat in front of that cold, white, blank screen on the computer.

Daddy can skip a flat rock across a rippling lake so that it turns to a bunny and hops across the top, as quick as can be, before it settles to its new burrow under the water. I like to think those rocks grow ears and tails under there, dart around fish and past nets in wonderment at going from a lonely life as a rock with just one view in all its days to skipping across the lake, swallowing up its magic, and turning to a merbunny.

Wouldn't you know it? My legs pressed together and feet flopped out like a fish tail, and my bedroom sunk to the bottom of the lake. I glubbed and blubbed past my books, in circles atop my desk chair, and then up to flop onto my bed.

So, there I was, seemingly jumping on my bed, when Daddy came in to check on my progress.

"Trixy Mae." He crossed his arms.

"I'm developing a plot," I whispered, cheeks still puffed out even as my merbunny tail dissolved into two plain old legs underneath me.

"It's almost bedtime." Daddy leaned in the doorframe, arms still crossed.

I blubbed once more. Daddy shut the door.

I could stitch together a story about a merbunny, no problem. But Mrs. Brown wanted something true. While I couldn't *prove* that skipped rocks didn't turn into merbunnies—*and neither could that turtleneck-loving, fact-checking* . . . I shushed that uncharitable part of my soul and focused on that blank screen.

A story bloomed behind my eyes, one Gran had whispered to me in the dark when I had similar feelings of not being enough.

Chapter Six

In the days that followed, I wrote all about Gran fleeing across the great state of Tennessee. About her plucking honey right from a hive. I pulled the stories from deep inside where they were supposed to have settled under a wispy cover of Gran's wishes.

Every time I turned in a story, my ears buzzed and buzzed.

Mama tried to tell me I got water in them from being a merbunny in the tub. Daddy said maybe the ringing in his ears wasn't from the quarry blasting; maybe it was genetic. "You'll get used to it," he said. Nurse Bev looked down the tunnels of my ears and declared them dandy. "It's just in your head. It'll fade." Of course it was in my head! Weren't all ears in people's heads?

They were all wrong. I knew what was making my ears ring. Gran, reminding me that I had no right to these stories, warning me that they weren't going to be heard the way they ought.

I kept one story buried at the bottom of a deep, deep ocean that I would not touch. One that Gran told me on accident, when it rose inside her and leaked through her eyes and out of her mouth. One she told like it would drown her if she didn't. One that ended with three words: *Hush, Trixy. Hush.*

That story I'd keep.

I thought again about those rocks Daddy had skipped over the lake. What had really happened when they finally stopped dancing. They sank.

Every time I snagged one of Gran's stories, she stirred the air around me. Warning me to listen up, to remember her, to keep my promises. But for reasons I didn't fully understand, each time I sat in front of a ghost-blank screen, I filled it with Gran's words.

Maybe it was because somewhere in the middle of putting those tales into straight lines of black and white, I'd hear Gran whispering into my ear. My fingers flew across the keyboard, sticking those words into permanent place, and for a few moments, she'd be real, standing behind me. I sometimes thought I could see her reflection in the screen if I squinted hard enough. She was the realest thing I had in those moments. So much realer than Mama, who would crumble if I hugged her, who seemed to disappear into her suddenly baggy clothes, who seemed never to eat or to sleep, who maybe was the real ghost.

Every time I handed those pages over to Mrs. Brown, ears ringing and heart hammering, I was filled with guilt. But also with sparks of something else. Maybe happiness? Maybe joy? Maybe not everyone heard the stories the way I had or Gran intended; but still, they heard them. They remembered her. They were thinking about *Gran.*

Mama and Daddy were the only other ones who really knew her, and I couldn't talk to Mama any more than I could tell Gran I was sorry.

Mama wasn't there. And Gran wasn't answering, so that didn't leave me a lot of options for chitchats. Daddy was around, of course, but he only heard the loud. I don't just mean because of his ringing ears. I mean, in general, he only picked up the loudest thoughts I had, and those, he'd hold in his big hands and try to reshape. He didn't seem to *hear* me.

Most of my thoughts these days were quiet.

Those weren't the only changes.

Mrs. Brown was different. She had started taking piano lessons with the music instructor during lunch and after school. All day, she hummed music. Her fingers drummed as she read my latest story. The biggest difference was her smile. She smiled all the time now.

Miranda, sucking on her hair again, turned around as I slipped into the seat behind her. "Catrina Alfonso hates you."

"Good morning to you too, Miranda," I snapped. "My, how I hope you have a pleasant day."

Miranda had a satisfied look on her face. The only time she looked that way was when she was stirring up trouble. The rest of the time, she buckled herself tight, pulling her hair into her mouth so only her little eyes and a patch of face showed.

"I don't even know Catrina Alfonso. I think you have me mixed up with someone else."

"Catrina is Mrs. Alfonso's daughter—you know, the *librarian*? That means she's the best writer in the whole school." Miranda rolled her eyes like she couldn't believe my ignorance. "Mrs. Brown was bragging about you to Mrs. Alfonso, saying that you wrote the best story the other day. Anyway, that's just not possible because everyone knows Catrina is the best writer. She even went to a summer camp in Pennsylvania just for kids who write good."

Someday I will have inner fortitude not to correct

Miranda Sherman's grammar, but today was not that day. "She writes *well*, not good."

Miranda stuck out her tongue at me. "You think you're so much better than the rest of us. But you aren't. Catrina's won every short story contest the library ever held. She'll win this one too."

"I don't have any idea what you're talking about, Miranda Sherman. I think you've sucked up too much shampoo, and it's affected your brain."

Miranda leaned forward and, wouldn't you know it, that slug hair slapped against the bare skin of my arm. I don't think I will ever recover. I shuddered, but she didn't notice. "I'm talking about the Happened-to-Me story contest! Every year, Catrina wins and then gets to write another story for the regional round. Someday she'll win that one too, and then she'll write a third for the state contest. *This* year, Mrs. Brown says she's entering *your* stories."

"Trixy, you did it again!" Mrs. Brown clapped her hands together as I stood next to her desk. "Tell me," she said, her brown eyes locked on mine. "Is it true? Everything in here?"

"True as my hair is curly."

"Excellent," she said. "I have some news for you. Exciting news!"

"You're entering me in a story contest," I said. "The Happened-to-Me one at the library."

Mrs. Brown's forehead wrinkled. "How did you guess?"

I shrugged.

"You could win a scholarship, Trixy! No one from our little town has ever made it past regionals, but I think you have a solid shot." Her wide smile wavered at my lack of enthusiasm.

"Who's going to read the stories?"

"The judges," Mrs. Brown said. "So, for our library, it would be Mrs. Alfonso. Then you would be asked to send that story *and* another one to the regional contest."

"I'd rather not," I said, and turned to head back to my seat. "Thank you anyway."

"Trixy, I already spoke with your parents. Well, with your dad. He was very excited to hear about the scholarship!" Mrs. Brown tilted her head at me. Her face flushed a pinkish color I had never seen on her before. "I think you should know, your stories are quite good." She picked at the sleeve of her shirt and for a moment her chin disappeared as she tucked it in. "Some might even say life changing."

Chapter Seven

About a week before I ran away with Raymond Crickett, a story about Gran played in my mind. It spun like the ballerina inside a music box Daddy had given me for my sixth birthday. Around and around and around.

I crawled out of my bed, tugging my sheet off the mattress and around my shoulders, to type the story in the middle of the night, thinking if I put it down in straight rows on the paper, it might stop circling my mind.

Dollie and Lil Sis knew better than to ask where they'd be headed when Mother and Father said to get in the car. "Life's too big to be stuck in one spot," Mother was fond of saying. The girls trusted she and

Father had a plan, knew the destination even if the girls weren't privy to it.

After two days of driving across the Smoky Mountains, Father parked the car in front of a small brick house in a row of small brick houses in Wayward, Tennessee, a little town on the outskirts of Nashville. A boy passed by on his bike. He paused, mouth hanging open, as he watched the girls step from the car and smooth their hair, and then pedaled off.

A woman opened the screen door and stood in the doorway, arms crossed. Her hair was a poof of tight brownish-gray curls. "What's going on now?" she said. "I done told you–"

But when Dollie and Lil Sis rounded the car, the sight of them was a hot iron smoothing the scowl of her face. Mother pushed Lil Sis ahead. The woman squatted, both arms out so wide Dollie could feel the warmth of her heart beating out toward them. "Come here to your Aunt Elise!"

Again, Mother nudged Lil Sis between her shoulder blades, pushing her into the arms of the woman. Dollie stepped backward toward Father, who tipped her forward as well when the woman kept her arms wide enough for both sisters. "Oh, sweet girl,"

Aunt Elise said, her nose pressed against Dollie's cheek so that her words were a tickle. "I haven't seen you since you were knee high to a grasshopper." Her hug was tight and soft all at once. The woman smelled like lemons and lavender, and her hair was bristly against Dollie's cheek. When she finally pulled back, Dollie didn't know if her cheeks were wet with the woman's tears or her own. Aunt Elise's eyes darted back and forth across Dollie's face.

The woman rose and squeezed Lil Sis's shoulders, introducing herself as Father's aunt. "And you," she said, turning to Dollie, "what a beauty you've become." Her hands went to Dollie's head, then glided down her hair to gently tug at one of her dark corkscrew curls. She pulled it and watched it bounce.

Mother cleared her throat, and Father stepped forward. "We can only stay the night, Elise. Just wanted the girls to see some kin." The adults stared at each other a beat too long.

Dollie looked down at Lil Sis and gave a little nod. *There's a story we can't hear.*

Aunt Elise's face shuttered. She didn't respond to Father, just nodded to the girls. "I bet you're tired," she said, and ushered them inside. "I'm afraid I don't have clothing–"

"They have clothes," Mother piped up.

Aunt Elise didn't pause. "There are towels in the cupboard. Why don't you wash up in the bathroom?"

That night Dollie and Lil Sis slept in a bed with cool, clean sheets covered in a print of cowboys. Late in the night, the door to the room cracked open. Dollie sat up and rubbed at her eyes. Mother's slim hand beckoned Dollie toward her. Were they off to another adventure? Would Lil Sis be left behind in this house with showers and sheets and warm hugs?

Dollie followed Mother down the hall and out the front door. The night was crisp with a yellow moon and bright pricks of starlight. Mother smiled and tweaked Dollie's chin with her long fingernails. "Your great aunt is right, Dollie," she said. "You are becoming a beauty." She gestured for Dollie to sit beside her on the porch. "Part of that is your curls. I know a way to make them even bouncier."

Dollie's face burned. Her aunt's compliment that morning had been a fire blazing away inside her, one that she had been tamping down and trying not to stand too close to in her mind. No one had ever called her a beauty before and now both Aunt Elise *and* Mother had done so. Mother, always elegant with her hair perfect and lips red, would know what made someone beautiful.

From the pocket of her long trench coat, Mother pulled out a pair of shiny scissors. "We'll trim those curls, and when Father and I come back they'll be bouncier than you could believe."

"When you come back?" Dollie shivered, both from the cool metal of scissors at her neck and the idea of being left behind.

Snip, *snip*, *snip* went the scissors. *Silly to be worked up about either*, Dollie told herself, trying to push the sad, scared parts of herself into the curls falling to her feet. She just had to believe that Mother had a plan.

"I can't get them to be even. Hold still, Dollie!"

Snip, *snip*, *snip*.

Mother sighed and brushed the dark curls from her lap. "Oh, well," she said. "It'll grow back." Dollie ran her hand along her scalp, feeling hair shorter than Father's. Mother shrugged. "I suppose your sister is the beauty now."

Mother went inside, but Dollie stayed on the porch under the stars, hoping the cement under her would grow cold enough to numb. *What's wrong with you?* she asked herself. *You don't need those hurt feelings any more than you need those curls. It's just hair.* But for a few hours that day, she had been beautiful.

Dollie returned to bed when she heard the car engine turn.

In the morning, Aunt Elise's face faltered for just a moment when she saw Dollie. And then she exclaimed that she had a lovely ribbon she never wore.

Dollie didn't want to go outside to play with Lil Sis, not even with the red silk bow atop her head. But Aunt Elise's eyes filled with tears whenever she saw Dollie, so out she went.

When the boy on the bicycle pedaled by, Dollie straightened her back. He paused and, though Dollie wanted to duck her head, she kept her chin high. "Are you a movie star?" the boy asked.

Lil Sis giggled but Dollie just winked at him. "Yes. Have you seen my limousine?"

Aunt Elise came out onto the porch and the boy rode away. "Don't you tease that boy," she said. "The Michaelson family's been through a lot, Henry the most of all." She smoothed Dollie's ribbon. "Besides," she said, "they're our bread and butter." Aunt Elise worked at the Michaelson Canning Factory, making cans of vegetables and beans.

Lil Sis clapped her hands. "My sister," she said, "the movie star."

When Gran told me this story so many years ago, I had gasped.

Gran had smiled and cupped my pointy chin in her palm. "It was only hair." She shook her head, dispersing a river of silvery gray hair. "And it grew back."

"But was it curly?"

The river rippled over Gran's shoulders. "No, it was straight as truth after that."

I climbed onto her lap and rested my cheek against her shoulder and fluffed up my own hair so the wild tangle of curls covered us both.

Chapter Eight

Catrina Alfonso waited for me at the top of the stairs leading into Clarkville Primary School.

I knew she was looking for me because only pure bitter hatred could pucker someone's face so much. Plus, across the top of the printed white paper she held in her hand, I saw my name. Beside her was Miranda Sherman, sucking once more on her hair. Miranda elbowed Catrina as I stepped off the bus after Raymond Crickett.

"Trixy Mae Williams!" Catrina shouted.

Raymond scurried into the school.

"That's my name." I drew myself upward as tall as could be and looked Catrina in her mean little eyes. "What are you doing with my story? That was for Mrs. Brown."

"She gave this so-called story to my mother, who showed me." She leaned forward, towering even if she hadn't been on a step higher, both hands now clenched at her sides. "For the life of me, I have no idea why anyone thinks *you're* so special."

I sighed and pointed to a poster hanging by the entrance of the school. It showed a bunch of stick figure students. Around them were the words: *Here Everyone Is Special.*

Catrina stomped her foot. "Trixy, this story doesn't even make *sense.* It doesn't have a *lesson.* Everyone knows stories have to have *lessons.* You've got no business entering that writing contest. *I* enter it every year, and every year, I *win.*"

I shrugged. "It's just a story."

"Without a *lesson,*" Catrina blustered again. "Something has to break, something has to be fixed, and someone has to *learn a lesson.* No one learned a lesson in your story!"

And while Catrina stood there, foot stomped and eyes mean, wouldn't you know it? My ears began to buzz all over again. Just from her talking about my story! That buzzing soon turned into words. Catrina's voice, I realized, whispering a story I was sure she didn't want me to hear, one I probably shouldn't have heard.

Catrina sat in front of her closed bedroom door. On the other side of it, her mother curled up on a living room armchair, legs tucked underneath her as she slowly turned the pages of a book. A pile of books lay in a basket at her feet. Beside her, Catrina's father held out a television remote toward the big screen over the fireplace, flipping through channels. On the kitchen table was a broken vase.

"Can I come out yet?" Catrina yelled through the crack at the bottom of her door.

"You can come out once you've learned your lesson, Catrina," her father said.

I willed my ears to close like a garage door right in the middle of that story. I didn't need to feel sympathy for Catrina Alfonso, not when she was towering over me on those steps.

"I'm going to win that competition, Trixy!" Catrina growled. "No one would believe your silly story, anyway."

Poof! Sympathy gone.

"That's funny," I said, leaning on my back leg and smiling so wide it looked to the world that I was finer than a hair on a frog split three ways. "Mrs. Brown told me that no one from Clarksville ever got past regionals. She said *I* have a shot at going to state."

Catrina gasped and her hands flew to her cheeks, dropping my typed-up story in the process.

The pages drifted down to her feet and her ghost story floated out of my ears and into vapor.

I twirled my fingers in a good-bye as the bell rang, and I wasn't sure if it was to her or the story.

Fury might not make someone burst into for-real flames, but I swear my face singed as I bounced by her on the stairs.

Miranda turned in her seat later that day. Unlike her usual whipping around, this time she slowly slid to the side. She didn't even look at me, keeping her eyes on the speckled tiles of the classroom floor instead.

"Did she really look like a movie star?" Miranda whispered. Technically speaking, we were supposed to be working on our math problems. Mrs. Brown was at the front of the room, wiping down the whiteboard as piano music poured from the speaker on her computer. Most everyone had their arms folded into bony pillows and were thinking through those problems with their eyes closed. Raymond Crickett even had a line of drool drip, drip, dripping off the side of his desk.

"Who?" I picked up the worksheet.

Now Miranda did look at me. "Without that hair," Miranda said. "Did she look like a movie star? Dollie, I mean."

All the air in the room *whooshed* out the window as she lifted some wrinkled pages. My story.

I looked at Miranda, and again my ears buzzed. I breathed as it settled into a different story.

Miranda stood in front of her bathroom mirror, hair wrapped in a towel after a shower. She smeared away the fog in a small circle, so she was the only thing reflected. She turned on the bathroom fan to cover her voice as she acted out scenes from her favorite movies. In that bathroom, in that mirror, she was the star.

The story ended with her unwrapping the towel from her head, her wet hair closing like a curtain around her face.

I pressed my hands against my ears, my mouth fish-flapping open.

"Well?" Miranda asked.

I shook my head, trying to clear it.

"That's what I thought," Miranda said, and ducked her head so her hair covered all but a pizza slice of her face. She twisted back in her seat.

"No," I yelped, coming back to my senses. I grabbed her wrist, so she'd turn back to me. "She always was beautiful. No matter what," I told both Mirandas.

Miranda faced front again, slinking forward to lay her head on her outstretched arm. "I wonder if it was scary, not having her hair like that."

I rested my chin on my fist and stared out the window as Mrs. Brown nudged the volume to cover Raymond's snores.

"I'm scared all the time," Miranda whispered.

"So was she," I said. "She told me that once, that she was scared all the time. She said brave doesn't have anything to do with being scared. Being brave is doing what you need to do while giving your scared feelings a bit of honey. Besides, it was just a little hair. She was still herself."

"That don't make no sense," Miranda said, her voice a little louder.

But remembering what Gran said about honey made me think of another story. I turned over the worksheet and wrote it right then and there. I pulled another and then another sheet from my backpack.

A little white cross surrounded by a knee-high fence perched at the far edge of the Michaelsons' farm.

Dollie asked about it as she and Henry, the boy who had called her a movie star, sat side by side swinging their legs on a giant weeping willow limb.

"I had a little sister too, and her name was Bea," Henry told her.

One day, when he and Bea were so small his mother could hold one on each hip, itchy red dots peppered Bea's neck. Henry pointed them out, and Bea had stuck out her tongue at him, a tongue covered in small white bumps. The next day, red dots marched across her chest and her back, then scurried right over onto him. "I got better," Henry told Dollie. "Bea didn't."

That was about when Henry's mom ran out of the house, her finger wagging at them, yelling, "Get down from that tree *right now*, Henry Michaelson!"

Something fell into place in Dollie's mind at that moment. She hadn't understood why Mrs. Michaelson was so angry all of the time. Now she knew she wasn't angry; she was scared. Scared that she'd lose Henry.

When Henry got too nervous or too loud or too busy, his lungs squeezed together. "Give me a minute," he would say, rubbing his knuckles over his ribs until those lungs stopped gripping each other.

Dollie found herself doing the same thing in that moment. Her lungs hadn't deflated, but something else cinched her chest. Something ugly and unwelcome. *Why did some parents hold their kids so close?*

Later that summer, as Dollie, Henry, and Lil Sis lay on their backs in the soft grass, Dollie asked Henry, "What do you want more than anything?"

"To be a traveling singer," he had said, the truth floating through him. "But it won't happen. My folks would never let it. I've got to take over the factory."

The next day, the girls had returned, this time

with Lil Sis holding a cowboy hat she and Dollie had found in Aunt Elise's guest closet.

Henry had worn it every day of this most exciting summer with Dollie and Lil Sis. The rest of the kids in the neighborhood never wanted to play with him, not with how his parents would show up and scold them for playing baseball with wooden bats. They mocked him, sometimes, for the way he rubbed at his chest.

Sometimes, Dollie caught herself mocking him too. Maybe that wasn't the right word. More like poking at him.

"We've had countless adventures," Dollie had told Henry. "So many we're frankly bored of them. That's why we're here with Aunt Elise. Just to be bored for a bit."

"Do you think *we* could have an adventure?" Henry had asked.

"I suppose," Dollie answered.

First, he, Dollie, and Lil Sis had tried to build a tree house, using pieces of wood stacked behind the barn or drug from the refuse piles. Henry's mom, her hands covering her mouth, screamed they'd get lockjaw. The next weekend, Henry's dad had built a perfectly square tree house with cemented posts surrounding the small oak just in front of the kitchen window.

For their second attempt at adventure, the three of them had stood on the loft of the old red barn in the backyard, flung out their arms, and fell like angels onto the mattress of hay spread below them. They had made sure the hay was freed from its bales, piling it up so that it was thicker than Lil Sis was high, but still Henry's parents had sent Lil Sis and Dollie home with a swat toward their bottoms. "Those girls are nothing but trouble," Henry's mom had said to their backs. "They should go back where they came from and leave you alone."

But Henry wanted to spend every minute with Dollie and Lil Sis. The girls had told him they wouldn't be there long, that their parents would be back soon from whatever new adventure they had sought out, and Aunt Elise would be just a memory. "A good one," Lil Sis had added in a mutter that only Dollie could hear. Dollie had scratched at her too-tight skin.

So this was to be their third and, though they did not yet know it, final attempt at pushing adventure into Henry's life. Adventure *and* proof to his parents that he was capable and brave.

Dollie and Lil Sis sat cross-legged in the grass, facing each other knee to knee.

"We can do it!" Lil Sis clapped her hands. "I know we can."

Dollie pushed her lips together, thinking through the plan. She turned to Henry, who sat beside his bicycle on the grass.

"*Or* we could wait for my parents to do it," Henry said. His cowboy hat covered most of his face. His brown eyes were wide and his face pale under the sprinkling of summer freckles across his nose.

"No! I watched your dad do it once. It was easy as pie," Dollie insisted. "Show them *you* can do things."

"It won't help," he said in his lonesome voice. "They don't take anything I do seriously."

Dollie pushed herself to her feet. "They think you don't know how to do things, Henry. You need to show them."

Dollie looked at the boy, at his carefully clipped hair, his clean clothes and freshly scrubbed skin. Behind her was his house, surrounded by lush grass and filled with couches with quilts and pictures in frames and bowls of food for everyone, even the little dog. She raised her chin. "If you show them that you're strong and brave and capable, maybe they'll trust you, the way our parents trust us."

Lil Sis's head whipped toward Dollie. In the month they'd been at Aunt Elise's, Lil Sis had grown an inch and gained five pounds, her sunken cheeks filling with sunshine and Elise's cherry cobbler. At night, sometimes Lil Sis padded from the bed they shared over to the one that was just hers, lying across the top of it like a starfish.

On those nights, Dollie pulled a wristwatch out from where she had slipped it under the mattress. Father had left it behind, right on top of the dresser, when he and Mother had packed to go. He probably left it by accident, as they had both departed in the middle of the night. But maybe he had done it on purpose, so she could lay it under her pillow and hear the *tick, tick, ticking* like his heartbeat.

Probably he left it because it was too big and ugly, Dollie thought on less happy nights.

I paused, my pencil over the paper I was scribbling this story on.

That *tick, tick, tick.* That was like the buzzing in my ears. The one that whispered other people's stories to me. The one that wouldn't let me forget Gran's stories. When I wrote those stories down, when I handed them to other people, Gran was with me. I missed her. I missed her down to my toes.

I missed Mama just as much. I wanted to tell *her* the stories. But even if I left them around the house, printed on paper I put on her dresser or fanned out on the table, she would never touch them.

Dollie's closely shorn hair lifted and fell across her forehead in the early summer breeze. She hadn't gotten taller or softer. Outside, she was the same size as ever. But something inside had snipped away to fall at her feet in dark curls. Doing everything the same every day—playing with Lil Sis, coming home to warm soup on the table and hot water in the bath—made her skin feel so tight she sometimes asked Lil Sis to check her back for splintering cracks.

Did Mother and Father trust them?

Beside her, Henry and Lil Sis started singing a silly song about making wishes on stars. Henry clapped out the beat on his knee and then pretended his bicycle wheel was a banjo he could pluck as Lil Sis danced around.

Soon Henry stood and bowed to Lil Sis, who curtsied back. He flicked his right foot behind him, leaned forward, and landed on it, then did the same on the other leg. He kept doing this little jig until Lil Sis got it too. Then he grabbed her arm and spun her around. Lil Sis twirled away, linking into Dollie's arm. "I'm not dancing," Dollie said. "We have to finalize our plan."

The two of them danced without her.

This third plan had begun when Dollie had noticed something while she was standing on that barn loft, just before she sent herself over the edge. A buzzing, all around her.

A beehive, built into the walls of the barn.

Later, she had watched Henry's dad as he moved about the farmhouse, and one day he had confirmed it. Henry's dad had donned a hat with a veil and lifted a little door at the bottom of the barn wall. Holding a small metal can, he pumped gray smoke into the wall. Suddenly, the bees' buzzing slowed. Using a small curved knife, he had cut a chunk of honeycomb right from the hive. He hadn't even worn gloves, just reached in and separated the bees. Some of them crawled across his fingers, but his movements were steady and calm.

He had chuckled when he heard Dollie gasping behind him. Dollie liked Henry's dad; he was tall and kind, with hands that he mostly kept in his pockets. He broke off a wedge of the honeycomb and handed it to her. Dollie had popped it into her mouth, chewing the comb and sending sweet honey to warm her down to her core. "Weren't you scared?" she asked as he placed the rest of the comb, dripping with honey, into a glass jar.

Henry's dad had shrugged. "Honey's worth the sting."

Henry's dad told her that it used to be somewhat common for farmers to foster bees, prompting them to nest inside the walls of a house or barn, building honeycombs in the space between the studs. This barn wall was built specifically for it, down to the little door at the bottom of the wall.

"What's in the can?" she had asked.

Henry's dad had knelt in the grass and opened the smoker lid. Inside was smoldering newspaper. "The smoke calms the bees. It blocks their main way of talking to one another—through smell. So they stop trying to protect their family and just take care of themselves."

Since that day, Dollie, Lil Sis, and Henry had spent the early mornings with their ears pressed against the barn. They had heard buzzing up the entire length of the wall. The hive must've been about twenty feet high.

Two days earlier, when Mr. Michaelson left the smoker can out in the barn, Dollie hatched a plan.

Here it was: While Henry's parents were out visiting his grandma, Henry and Dollie would drape a sheet over themselves, holding it so it pinched under their chins just like a veil. Then Henry would yank open the door and Dollie would use a butter knife she had pilfered from Aunt Elise during breakfast to lob off a chunk of honeycomb. Lil Sis would stand back, peeking under a second sheet, holding the smoker and wafting it toward the bees. She would warn them if the bees didn't seem to be in a sharing mood.

Dollie shouted the details of the plan over Henry's singing and Lil Sis's giggles.

"What if they chase us?" Henry bowed to Dollie, who sighed and curtsied.

"We crush them!" Lil Sis clapped her hands together, going off beat, as Henry twirled Dollie around.

"No!" Dollie and Henry said at the same time. Dollie tried to stop dancing, but Lil Sis linked through her other arm. She and Henry kept dancing, pulling her along.

"We run." Dollie tilted her head toward the little pond just beyond the barn. "Bees don't like water."

"How do you know?" Henry asked.

"I just do." Dollie, in fact, did not know for certain this was true. Lil Sis twirled away, singing and clapping, leaving her and Henry's arms linked.

"What if we get stung?" Henry turned so now they faced each other, his hand on her waist and the other holding her hand out to the side.

"The honey will be worth the sting." She ducked under his arm and let his hand drop.

Soon, Henry's parents left, walking down the long driveway toward his grandmother's house in town. Dollie, Lil Sis, and Henry silently watched until Mr. and Mrs. Michaelson disappeared.

The three of them gathered by the little door, ears pressed against the wood. The buzzing on the other side wasn't as loud as when they had checked the day before. Most of the bees were probably out gathering pollen.

They went over the details so many times that Henry figured they only had a half hour at most before his parents returned. "Just think of when they come home to see us chewing on honeycomb," Dollie said, even though it made Henry's face paler.

Lil Sis draped the sheet over Dollie and Henry. They stood so close that Dollie felt Henry shaking. He was a bit taller than her; Henry's shoes peeked below the sheet, along with a sliver of his black socks. Beside them, Lil Sis stood at the ready, her sheet-covered hands holding the can filled with burning newspaper. "Now," Dollie barked, and Lil Sis began pumping the smoke toward the little door.

They could see through the thin fabric of the sheet, though the smoke made it tougher. Henry placed one quaking finger on Dollie's back. Lil Sis's outstretched hand began to raise the little door. The bees' buzzing seemed to be the beginnings of a scream. Lil Sis stepped backward half a step but kept pumping the smoke into the hive. A few dozen bees circled around them, crawling along their huddled forms inside the sheet. Dollie breathed steadily in and out, in and out.

The opening in the door revealed long, thin strips of honeycomb the color of fresh garden corn, dripping with honey. With a steady sheet-draped hand, she reached into the comb. Here she hesitated. *Would it destroy their home? Would she cut through a bee?*

"Hurry!" Henry urged, his hand hovering over the door, ready to slam it shut. The sheet rippled between them, showing his skinny ankles.

Dollie licked her lips, then began to saw at the middle honeycomb.

The bees climbed along her covered hands and hopped out of the way of the knife. Henry whimpered beside her. Lil Sis kept pumping the smoke, stepping backward inch by inch as more bees left their home to investigate. But somehow, Dollie wasn't scared.

The bees on her hands weren't frightening; they were curious. They seemed to know they *could* make it harder for her to slice away at their home, but perhaps practiced at not being in control, they didn't. She breathed in and out, in and out.

The chunk of honeycomb fell from the hive.

"Yes! We did it!" Henry said, and stretched to close the door.

And that's when everything went wrong.

Chapter Nine

Two seconds too late, Dollie remembered something else Mr. Michaelson had told her about bees.

"There aren't too many things that scare a bee, especially when she's got her buddies around. 'Bout the only thing that bothers them is bears, skunks, and raccoons. That's why I wear this getup." He had gestured to his white beekeeping suit. "They hate the color black. Reminds them of those predators."

Henry leaned forward to close the door.

They hate the color black.

An inch or so of Henry's black socks were exposed above his canvas sneakers. A bee zoomed toward it, landing on the skin just above the sock.

"Yow!" Henry screamed and kicked his foot. Sure enough, the shoe went flying, and now his whole socked foot was visible. The bees circled and then *attacked.*

Henry stumbled backward, screaming as his foot twisted when he tumbled over Dollie's legs.

"Run, run, *run!*" Dollie shouted, tossing the honeycomb to the ground and grabbing Henry around the waist. She yanked him backward as he yelped. Lil Sis rushed forward, screeching as she pumped more smoke toward the stream of bees. But by then the newspaper had incinerated, and nothing came out of the little hose. Lil Sis threw the whole can at the bees, and then wrapped her arm around Henry's other side. The three of them barreled forward, chased by bees, the sheets flapping behind them, toward the pond.

And it was at that moment—when the sisters appeared to be dragging a wailing, sheet-draped Henry to his imminent drowning—that Henry's parents headed up the driveway.

The trio didn't pause, plunging right into the water.

That was the last time Dollie saw Henry for a very long time.

Two weeks later, Aunt Elise told her and Lil Sis she couldn't take care of them anymore, not with the trouble they were making in town. "I can't make ends meet with two more kids as it is," she said, tears streaming down her red cheeks. "I work at the Michaelsons' factory. They said they'd fire me. They threatened to sue me for all I've got—which is just this house."

Twelve stingers had to be pulled from Henry's foot. Due to the way Henry twisted his ankle as he ran, the doctor wasn't entirely sure that he'd ever walk without a limp. Aunt Elise told them all of this as they sat on top of small suitcases filled with clothes Aunt Elise herself had folded into rectangles. They waited for the orphanage worker to collect them. Aunt Elise hadn't been able to track down Mother or Father.

Lil Sis cried, but Dollie just stared ahead as Aunt Elise answered a knock on the door.

It wasn't the orphanage worker at the door. Instead, wrapped in a small cloth on the doorstep was a little chunk of honeycomb. A note, the edges sticky with honey, was pinned to the top. *Worth the sting. ~H.*

"What happened next, Trixy?" Mrs. Brown asked me the next day, grabbing my shoulders to keep me from passing by her in the hall. The nice, neat, typed version of the story I had scribbled all over my math worksheets the day before was tucked under her arm. "Were they really sent to an orphanage?"

I didn't answer, just unzipped my backpack and pulled out another stack of papers for Mrs. Brown. "You can read all about it here."

Mrs. Brown dropped my shoulders and took the story. Today, she wore a skirt covered in piano music print.

"Oh, Trixy, I just love what a natural storyteller you are!" She hugged the papers to her chest. "I can't wait to share these with the story committee."

"I think we're all caught up now," I said, rubbing at my ears. "So you won't be needing more stories, right?"

Mrs. Brown's bottom lip puckered out. "Oh, but you could continue. I'd give you *extra* credit, you know."

Someone rammed into me from behind. I didn't need to turn around to know who it was: Catrina Alfonso.

"Miss Alfonso!" Mrs. Brown said. "Apologize. You nearly knocked Trixy over."

With her chin up in the air like that, Catrina seemed to be sixteen feet tall. "I'm sorry I *nearly* knocked you over."

"What has gotten into you, Catrina?" Mrs. Brown asked.

But whatever she would've said was shocked silent by an unexpected event.

Raymond Crickett, unloading his backpack into his locker, was first to spot it. He dropped his metal lunchbox to rattle onto the floor. "*Whoa,*" he gasped.

In front of me, Catrina's mouth popped open and her eyes bugged, her mean little words dashed away.

Next to me, Mrs. Brown's face underwent the same transformation.

As I turned around, I wasn't sure what I'd see—a hippopotamus trotting down the hallway, a tentacled alien sucking the brains of classmates, the principal on roller skates—any of these seemed like possibilities.

What I wasn't expecting was Miranda Sherman.

She wasn't trudging ahead, sucking on a chunk of hair and lurking behind someone more popular or angrier than her.

No, this Miranda Sherman stood tall in a bright pink dress. Her brown hair was clipped close to her head in a fluffy haircut Mama called a pixie cut. In fact, Miranda Sherman and Mama might've had the same stylist, since Mama came home a couple of days ago with the same look—only on Miranda it was different. Mama just looked smaller, but Miranda was sophisticated.

Miranda even wore a pair of big, dark sunglasses, though we were inside the school. "Hello." Her voice was cool as lemonade as she moved between us.

"Miranda!" Catrina yelped. "What happened to you?"

Miranda turned and lowered her sunglasses just a bit to peek over the top. "It's just a little hair."

And with that Miranda the Movie Star took her seat.

Catrina stomped her foot. Her face boiled tomato red. Her hands fisted at her sides. "Stop it!" she screamed to me. "You stop it right now, Trixy Mae Williams!"

"Stop what?" I threw my hands in the air. "I didn't cut her hair."

"Your stories!" she screamed. "You keep making up stories, and they keep changing people! Mrs. Brown, my mom, *you*. And now Miranda! It's wrong! *Wrong*." She stomped again. "And they're not even *real*!"

Catrina turned and stormed down the hall.

Mrs. Brown turned toward me with her eyebrows raised. "Is that true, Trixy?"

I nodded. The stories *were* changing everything.

"You made them up?" Mrs. Brown's forehead wrinkled as she shook her head. "But you were told they had to be *true* stories."

"They *are* true." I forgot myself for a moment, looking for all the world like a mini Catrina as I stomped. "She's wrong! Gran told me they're true!" My ears tingled.

"Can you prove it?" Mrs. Brown glanced down the hall to where Catrina was retreating. "Catrina seems put out about the stories you've been writing. Mrs. Alfonso told me this morning that the regional judges for the story contest called indicating *someone* anonymously suggested some entries might not be nonfiction."

"Yes." *Could* I prove that what Gran told me was the straight truth? It seemed in that moment that the only real proof was buried under the lilac bushes. Even so, I added, "I *will* prove it."

And wouldn't you know it? At that moment the buzzing in my ears settled and stopped.

"That's *it*!" I told Raymond on the bus ride home that afternoon. "That's what Gran's been tugging at me to do. *Prove* her stories! Do you know what this means? I had it all wrong! All this time, I thought she was angry with me for sharing them, but really she *wants* people to hear them! She wasn't fussing me; she was cheering me on."

Raymond nodded but he wasn't listening to me, not really. I knew that because he wasn't blinking or asking any questions, just staring and occasionally nodding that big head of his. He glanced behind him at his sister. Today, Sara wasn't asleep like usual. She was sitting upright with her blue hair piled atop her head, her eyes drifting from side to side. I wasn't sure if she could see him from where she sat on the bus, but she seemed to nod in his direction.

"Raymond Crickett," I snapped, "I'm having a moment here. Are you following along or not?"

"Not." He bent and pulled his backpack up from between his legs. "I mean, I heard you say you were all wrong, and I'm inclined to believe that's the truth." I gasped, but he ignored me, continuing to dig through his overstuffed bag, papers spilling out the sides and onto the dark green bus floor, where they slip-slided to mulch under other students' feet. He tugged out a small cluster of bent worksheets. *My* math worksheets, with Gran's bee story on the back.

"Hey! You—"

But Raymond interrupted me. "I pulled these from the recycling bins."

"You *swiped* them!"

Raymond didn't deny it. "I leave tomorrow after school, Trixy. For two weeks, with Sara and my dad for his tour."

"So?" I crossed my arms. "Besides, don't you think it's kind of mean to be talking about that trip when I don't get to go along like I was supposed to?"

"The honey is worth the sting," Raymond muttered, his cheeks suddenly pink.

"What are you talking about?" I narrowed my eyes.

"Before I go, I need to tell you something." Now Raymond's cheeks were splotchy red. He rubbed at his heart. "Some feelings I've been having."

Oh, stars. "No, you don't." I turned to face the front of the bus.

"Trixy," he said anyway. "I need you to know something."

"Sometimes I wish I had ear lids," I muttered.

"I like you," he said. "I like you even though you're mean to me."

"Don't be a dum-dum, Raymond," I said. "I'm not—"

"This story taught me something. Dollie's a jerk."

"What? I don't think you read the story right." I grabbed for the papers, but he twisted them away from me. "She's *not* a jerk," I said. "It's all about her trying to *help* Henry."

"No." Raymond shook his head, and his fingers tightened around the papers.

"My gran was the nicest person who ev—"

"Maybe when she was your gran," Raymond said, his voice soft, "but when she was Dollie, she was mean to Henry. She used him because he was nice to her, and she thought he'd always be there no matter what." His mouth formed words I don't think he meant me to hear. *Worth the sting.*

I glanced behind us to Sara, who now leaned forward in her seat, a little smile on her mouth.

"*You* are mean, Trixy. You're mean to me. Sometimes I even see you *thinking* meanness at me," he said. "Maybe it makes you feel better to do that, but it makes me feel worse. You should stop. And if you don't"—he gulped—"then I won't like you anymore."

He turned to face forward, and then added, completely unnecessarily, "And neither one of us has too many friends, so you ought to think about that."

For a moment, my brain was a crochet hook trying to pull at my wispy thoughts and yank them back into line. My plan for proving Gran's stories kept slipping away, replaced by the bitter truth Raymond was risking a sting to tell. I wanted to argue that he was wrong, that I was a lot of things, but mean wasn't one of them.

But I couldn't.

The bus rumbled to our stop. Raymond squeezed past me and left, my worksheet papers still on the seat. I started to get out, but Sara blocked my path. "He's right, and you know it," she said. I stood but she didn't move. "I haven't said anything to you because I know how much it can mess someone up when someone leaves them." Sara's pale cheeks turned pink the way Raymond's often did. "But you haven't been a good friend to him. He lost Gran too. We all did."

Sara glared at me a second, her eyes flickering back and forth, and then she followed him off the bus.

Instead of going to my house, I ran down the street to catch up with Raymond.

"I'm sorry."

Raymond stopped, though Sara didn't. I looked into Raymond's face, noticing his big brown eyes and the tilt of his head. I hated the idea of Raymond not liking me anymore, though I hadn't given him a reason to be my friend. Shame weighed down my head. "I haven't been a good friend to you lately."

"Not since Gran died," Raymond said.

My ears tingled as I once more heard a story. But this wasn't just Raymond's story; it also was mine.

It was from when Raymond and I used to be friends, real friends. This was a story about Raymond, waiting for me on the bus the day after his mother left. Of me walking up those stairs, looking around, and finding his eyes already on mine. Of how Raymond felt like all his heart's tiny cracks were coated in glue and sealed shut when I skipped down the aisle and sat beside him on purpose.

Then another part of the story, one that made me cover my ears with my forearms, not wanting to hear it. It was from after Gran died, the day I came back to school. Of Raymond sitting on his usual seat, staring at me with hot tears flowing down his soft cheeks, of his heart aching for me even though he loved her too. And how my face twisted, and I turned from him to sit right behind the bus driver.

The story stopped, and I gasped.

I don't know why, but I hated Raymond that day for no reason at all, except that his heart hurt for mine.

"I'll do better," I whispered.

Raymond smiled, and I smiled back.

I cleared my throat. "Want to come to my house? We can have some lemonade and . . ." I almost said we could work on my plan to prove Gran's stories, but it occurred to me that a good friend wouldn't make everything just about her, would she?

"Yes," Raymond said anyway. "I'd like that very much. Sara!" he yelled ahead to his sister. She turned. "I'm going to Trixy's house!"

Chapter Ten

Raymond's suggestion to figure out if Gran's stories were true was to ask Mama. And if that had worked, I never would've had to run away with him.

But I had doubts on the success of this plan for two big reasons. First, Gran made it raindrop clear that *I* was the only one who had ever heard her stories. Second, Mama didn't talk about Gran. Every time Daddy or I mentioned her, Mama seemed to shrink.

Even so, I asked Raymond to stay for dinner so we could try. We were having spaghetti and meat sauce with loaves of crusty garlic bread and a salad. The whole house smelled cozy and happy, and for all the world it looked to Raymond that this was how my family always had dinner together.

And that used to be the truth.

Before.

Gran used to make almost all our meals. Oatmeal or eggs for breakfast. Sandwiches at lunch. Dinner always had been like this—lots of dishes, steam rising from them. Mama used to tell Gran that she didn't have to make so much, that we could keep it simple with leftovers. But Gran loved watching everyone eat. As soon as a plate was empty, she'd lean over and add another dollop. She said cooking was the least she could do, since Mama and Daddy let her live with them in the little bedroom off the kitchen.

Mama always rolled her eyes at that, and Daddy told her he loved having her; she didn't have to earn her keep like that. But Gran just would disappear into the kitchen and reappear with more food.

Lately, Mama couldn't quite make it to dinner with the rest of us, drifting to and from the kitchen as Daddy and I ate, gathering salad dressings, salt, and extra napkins. Or she'd leave dinner on the stove top altogether and tell us to eat when we were hungry. Sometimes Daddy asked her to join us, at least so we could say grace, and then she'd sit between us. Only mostly she just pushed the food around her plate. Mama had never been big, but now? She was so skinny it scared me to hug her. Sometimes at night, Daddy's voice would drift out their bedroom window and into mine, and I'd hear him tell Mama that she was exercising too much and eating too little. That she needed help. Mama would tell him he didn't know what he was saying. Once she even yelled, saying Daddy didn't know what he was talking about, and went down to sleep on the couch.

Today, since Raymond was joining us, Mama sat at her seat between me and Daddy, and smoothed her napkin on her lap. Daddy smiled so wide I could see the silver filling in his molar glinting in the kitchen light. "Well, help yourself," Mama said after Raymond offered grace.

We passed around the bowl of pasta and basket of bread. Mama even took a few bites of spaghetti, twirling a noodle around and around on her fork. Her wrist was thinner than mine.

I licked my lips, then jumped right into the deep end of the ocean between Mama and everyone else. "Gran would've loved this dinner," I said. Mama didn't react. "Was there anything she *didn't* like to eat?"

I meant it as a joke. If there was one thing Gran loved near as much as me, it was food. Every meal she had, from a soft-boiled egg over toast to a slice of pizza from the restaurant in town, was "the best I've ever had." Bad food, she said, was infinitely better than no food.

"Spinach," Mama said into the abyss.

I opened my mouth to respond, but Daddy beat me to it, asking Raymond where he'd be going on this year's tour.

"Oh, same as usual." Raymond wiped sauce off his chin. He ended up just smearing it around. "Memphis, to kick off, then Jackson. Couple of days around Nashville, onto Cookville, Crawford, Knoxville, Kingsport, then loop around through New Orleans. You know, the usual." As he spoke, Raymond's accent seemed to deepen, as his words seeped right on into each other.

"Sounds like a full trip," Daddy said.

"Yes, sir." He glanced at me and then back at his plate again. "We always hit those first few towns because of Gran."

"I forgot about that," Daddy said. "She helped your father get his first gigs, didn't she?"

Raymond nodded. "Yeah, she set it all up. One day she came to the porch and handed Dad a list of venues." He laughed. "Sara wanted to skip some of them this year, said she's tired of the same small towns, but Dad said no way. He says you can't forget where you come from."

I knew all of this—I had been with Gran when she had handed Mr. Crickett the list. "These are places I know would be lucky to have you," she had told him. Mr. Crickett told her he could never manage the kids and a tour, and Gran laughed. "Take them with you! It'd be good for y'all.

You don't know what you're capable of doing until you have to do it. Now you go, be a star. Maybe one day, take me and Trixy here with you down memory lane."

I closed my eyes, seeing a flare of lights and feeling a crash deep inside me. I shuddered. "Gran wanted to go this year," I blurted. "She was going to show me all of the places she knew nearby. We were talking about it that day, in the car. The day of the—" I slammed shut my mouth. When everyone turned toward me, I realized I was holding my fork too tightly in my hand. I dropped it, smoothing my sweaty palms on my lap. *Knock it off*, I ordered my hammering heart. *You're safe. You're fine.*

Mom's chair scraped as she stood. "I'm getting more water. Anyone need anything?"

We shook our heads. Raymond picked up his fork. "We do stop at some great little towns." He slurped another noodle. "Like Little Bass. That's my favorite, and it's the first stop. There's a diner with barbecue I dream about sometimes."

Daddy laughed, but his eyes stayed on the doorway Mama had disappeared behind.

As she re-entered, I said, "Gran used to live in Tennessee, didn't she, Mama?"

"She did." Mama sat but pushed her plate away.

Daddy cleared his throat. "Some of those names sound familiar. Didn't Gran mention Little Bass? Jackson rings a bell too."

Mama stood again. "I'm going to get more salad dressings."

"That's okay," Raymond burst in, mouth full of noodles. "I won't be having any salad, ma'am."

"Me either," I said, "and Daddy already has dressing on his salad." Mama sat back down. "Do you know where she lived? Maybe a place next to a farm?"

"A farm?" Daddy echoed. "I don't remember Dolcie mentioning living on a farm."

"Oh, no." I shook my head. "*She* didn't live on the farm. A boy in town did. One day, she and Lil Sis even convinced him to help her break off a chunk of honeycomb straight from a beehive that soared all the way up the side of his barn. Can you believe it?"

But before Daddy could say that he for sure could not, Mama stood. "*Lil Sis?* My mother was an only child. My only family."

"That's not true!" I said.

Daddy cleared his throat. "You have us, Jenny."

"Right." Mama winced. She stepped softly from the kitchen and went to the bathroom, closing the door behind her with a click.

"Well," Raymond said. Daddy was in the kitchen, washing the dishes, and we were on the porch pew swing. "That didn't work. Where's all Gran's stuff? When I wanted to know about my mother, my dad gave me a box of stuff she didn't take when she left. Pictures and clothes and a bottle of perfume." His cheeks were splotchy again. "She probably didn't like that perfume, since she left it."

The kitchen clock *tick, tick, ticked* behind us. Sometimes I smelled flowers around Raymond. "It smells great."

We went down into the basement, past where Mama was doing an exercise video, to the back, cement-walled section where we kept boxes of stuff. If we had anything of Gran's, it'd be tucked away here. Raymond and I lifted lids, mostly of Christmas decorations, and tried not to be distracted, but before long we both were humming, then singing carols.

We were doing a round of "Let It Snow" when I found it, up on the top shelf. I had to climb on top of my old playpen to reach. A shoe box, tied with ribbon.

My fingers made smudges in the thick dust. I touched the ribbon. It was faded and frail.

"Red silk," Raymond whispered, "like the story."

I squinted at him, and Raymond's cheeks pinked. "Miranda let me see the story about Gran's hair." He sat beside me, close enough that his arm brushed mine.

Was this ribbon proof? It was to me, but maybe not to Mrs. Brown. Definitely not to Catrina Alfonso. We spread out all of the contents in a half circle around us. A sequin and feather, both black; a photograph; a small square of paper; a beat-up metal wristwatch; a couple of official-looking forms; a blue baby sock. Something hammered in my heart at that one, and I tucked it in my palm.

I picked up the photograph. It looked to be an all-girls school class picture. Each girl wore a black dress with a bib that buttoned at her shoulders over a long-sleeved white shirt. The girls had matching knee-high black socks. I pressed a finger over two children. These two girls stood side by side, the little one curled like a cashew toward the taller one, who glared into the camera, her chin high and her hair short. Below the picture was a label, printed: *The Society for Friendless Children, Little Bass, Tennessee. 1949.*

"Wow," Raymond said. "Your Gran was *old.*"

I glared at him.

He pointed to the sign in the picture. "The Society for Friendless Children. Sounds like us."

I crossed my arms. "We have friends, Raymond."

"Name seven." He snorted.

My mouth opened to prove him wrong and closed again when I couldn't.

Raymond cleared his throat. "Little Bass. That's the town with the diner! What a small world. I'll be there tomorrow!" Raymond licked his lips, no doubt thinking again on that barbecue. "This one time, I—"

"Little Bass?" I repeated, my heart hammering hard.

These are places I know would be lucky to have you. That's what Gran had said to Mr. Crickett about his tour. *These are places I know.*

Raymond squinted down at the picture. "Maybe I'll ask Dad to drive around. Maybe I'll spot this building."

I pulled the small square of paper toward me. The handwritten letters were faded, scrawled in a curling fashion I struggled to read. It seemed to have been handled so often most of the single sentence was rubbed away. But I recognized the dash and letter *H* at the bottom.

"Well, there you go! This is it," Raymond said. "The proof. Right there, that's Henry's letter."

I shook my head. "It's not *proof.* I don't *know* that this said anything about being worth the sting, nor that it was written by that Henry himself. I don't know that it's Gran in that class picture either." I sighed. "I know that these things *look* like they could prove Gran's stories, but they don't in themselves. Actually going there, talking to people who might've known Gran, only that would *prove* it enough to get to stay in the contest and not be in trouble with Mrs.

Brown, plus make Catrina shut her face. Maybe it'll even get Mama to . . ."

"Get your mama to what?" Raymond repeated, his voice soft as could be.

I shook my head, organizing my thoughts. "The orphanage is the first stop on the tour *Gran* arranged for your dad."

More splotches bloomed on Raymond's face. "Well, not the *orphanage*. I don't even think orphanages still exist. We're just going through that town. And then we'll be going across the state. The next spot is Jackson, and then we finish up the spots Gran arranged in Nashville before going on to new gigs Dad's band booked in Louisiana."

I went to the map of Tennessee Daddy had pinned to the wall, alongside Texas, Oklahoma, Louisiana, and Arkansas. On tiptoes, I leaned in, searching for Sweetheart Mountain, where once there had been a bakery that had served Liberace. There it was! Right next to Jackson. After that, he'd be going to Nashville. "Aunt Elise was near Nashville."

The whole time Raymond had been talking but I hadn't heard a word he said. ". . . but I don't know that . . . Why are your fingers twisting like that, Trixy? I think you're thinking thoughts you ought'n."

"You stop by *all* of the spots, Raymond!" I grabbed him by each shoulder. "*We* could go there and find proof!" I pointed to the half circle of mementos. "*Gran* created that tour, not just for your dad but for *her.* So that one day she could go back—*we* could go back—and she could show me the stories were true! *This* was going to be the year that we did. She said so, just before . . . Just before."

I realized I had the baby sock in my fist. I squeezed it as the story she had made me swear never to talk about again shifted under the silt of my promises.

The tour would prove the stories. If I had proof, then Mama would have to listen to me, listen to the stories. Maybe she'd hear the *tick, tick, tick* of Gran still with us. Maybe it'd even make Mama *Mama* again.

Chapter Eleven

If I was going to crash the Cricketts' tour, I had to think fast. Luckily, quick thinking runs deep in my bones.

Gran told me all about how savvy she could be.

On the first night at the Society for Friendless Children, Dollie and Lil Sis were lined up with a half dozen other new arrivals and given two dresses and one pair of shoes each. One by one, the girls were sent into a room to face Madame Brick, the director of the Society. The little old woman hummed from a rocking chair in the middle of the dimly lit, empty room, the rug under her seemingly the pelt of a long-passed shaggy animal. When Dollie was next in line, Lil Sis just behind her, she realized the rug wasn't made of fur. It was hair.

The old woman clutched a pair of shining silver scissors as a girl with hair to her waist stood in front of her. "We don't have any time for vanity at the Society," the old woman warbled. *Snip*, *snip*, *snip*, the hair fell around her.

Dollie whispered to Lil Sis, "You're going to look like a movie star just like me," when the woman beckoned her forward.

"I want to look like me," Lil Sis whimpered.

Dollie winked at her and then strode forward. She lifted her chin in the air and stared coolly at the woman, who stared right back with narrowed eyes. "No worries about vanity with you," the woman said, and pointed to Dollie's shorn hair.

"Likewise," Dollie snapped. The old woman's mouth dropped in the middle of her face. A whistling sound seeped from her. The woman was laughing, and it seemed to shock her as much as Dollie. She laughed so hard, she began to cough, face doubled over into her lap. Dollie gestured for Lil Sis to dart across the room to the other girls. That's how Lil Sis managed to keep her curls from adding to the old woman's rug.

At dinnertime, the children lined up tallest to shortest along benches on both sides of long tables. They were each given the same portions—a baked chicken thigh, a scoop of lentils, and two slices of apple. Dollie and Lil Sis, accustomed to eating whatever they were given, scraped up every bite. Lil Sis's feet swung back and forth while she ate.

After the meal, a woman's heels *clack, clack, clacked* as she paced the length of the two benches. She twisted the ears of girls who left lentils on their plates. While everyone else got to go outside, those girls stayed behind in the dining hall. A tall Black girl leaned toward Dollie. "They don't let you leave till you eat every bite," she whispered. "One time, a kid gagged so hard she threw up. They made her wash her plate and then they served her more of the same stuff." Her nose wrinkled. "I'm Sallie, by the way."

"Dollie. How long have you been here?" Dollie slipped into line behind Sallie as they left the dining hall. The women in charge didn't seem to mind if they talked, so long as they kept it quiet.

"About a year." The girl shrugged. "It's not so bad. Most days are finer than a frog hair split three ways. I've had worse Homes."

The way she said the last word, Dollie knew it didn't mean a place where someone lived with parents and a dog, the way Henry lived in a home. It was something else. Something with a capital *H*.

"They're strict about food." Sallie jerked her chin toward the girl in front of her, a thin girl with hair so red it looked like fire. When she turned to the side, Dollie saw that the girl's mouth was crumpled into itself. Her hands seemed to move like sticks at her sides, too stiff. "Jessa's the only one they don't bother about it. It's hard for her to chew."

"What happened?" Dollie asked.

Sallie's jaw set. "Like I said, some Homes are worse." She kind of laughed. "But it's good news if you're sitting next to her. Just slip some food you don't like onto her plate and the Clackers will leave you alone."

"Clackers?" Dollie repeated.

"That's what I call them," Sallie said with a shrug, and mimed stepping too hard on the ground. "Like I said, they're not bad, so long as you eat your food. That and don't make a lot of noise. If you've got a problem, figure it out or find someone to bargain with. Don't go to them."

"Well, I'll never have trouble with them." Dollie

grinned. "I love all food, and I've been taking care of myself my whole life."

Sallie snorted. "The Clackers will test you on that."

After dinner, the Clackers opened double doors to a playground filled with slides, basketball courts, and dozens of swings. Lil Sis skipped as she made her way to one in the middle, already holding hands with someone her size. Something twisted in Dollie, but just for a second, then Sallie nudged her side and handed her a jump rope.

Behind them, inside the dining hall, children held their noses and swallowed lentils one by one.

Late that first night, Lil Sis crawled into Dollie's bed. A few beds down from them, someone sniffled. Another child cried. They probably once had a home with a lowercase *h*.

"I miss Aunt Elise," Lil Sis whispered. She spread her still-long hair out on the pillow, making a soft blanket on the thin pillowcase.

"Are you kidding?" asked Dollie, thumbing over a bee sting hump on her wrist. "We have a whole playground! And did you see all that food for dinner?" She nestled farther into the bed. "We've got all we need, without that ole Aunt Elise and her silly neighbors."

"What about Henry?"

"We've got everything we need."

Straight into Dollie's ear, Lil Sis whispered, her warm breath making it tingle, "We're Rockefellers for sure."

I handed this story to Raymond on the bus the next morning, prepping to let him know I was serious about joining him on the road trip. He read it silently, then handed it back to me.

"Trixy, that story's sad," Raymond told me. "I don't think I like it much."

"You're not speaking sense. It's a happy story. Dollie and Lil Sis loved the Society for Friendless Children." I cleared my throat, about to lay it on Raymond that I'd be joining him on the road trip. "And they also show how making quick, last-minute decisions—"

Raymond shook his head. "I don't believe they did love it there."

"They did! Gran laughed the whole time she told me about it." I sighed and crossed my arms.

I could almost see Gran's eyes glistening, the corners of her mouth twitching as she told me stories from her time there. I pulled another story out of my backpack. Clearing my throat, I read it to him aloud.

While some girls struggled in the Home, Dollie and Lil Sis took to it like merbunnies in a lake.

They knew to be clean and ready to go when the buses picked them up early in the morning to go to the public school. They knew not to bother trying to befriend the kids who lived in town. They knew to wash their stockings in the sink every night and hang them from their bedposts to dry until morning. They knew that if their shoes didn't fit, they shouldn't point it out to Madame Brick, who would twist their ears, but instead trade among themselves. They knew that on Saturday evenings, they'd gather in the gymnasium and watch a real movie projected on the wall—so long as they followed the rules.

And luckily there were only two of those. First rule: figure out problems without asking a Clacker. Second rule: clear your plate.

Simply knowing what was coming next was a certain kind of gift they'd never been given before.

And so everything was great.

Until the spinach.

Dollie loved all food; no matter what it was, it was better than not having it.

Lil Sis was the same, with one exception: spinach. She hated spinach even more than waking up to a headache. More than falling asleep with an empty belly.

At dinner on this fateful day, Dollie took her usual seat next to Sallie. Down at the end of the row with the other smaller kids sat Lil Sis. A Clacker strolled around the lines, scooping ladles of food onto each plate. Rice, beans, and *spinach*.

Dollie didn't need to see Lil Sis's face to know her lip puckered at the sight. Her whole body recoiled from the soggy lump of stinky leaves.

And worst of all? This was Saturday, movie night. Tonight was going to be the best yet—a Disney film! Lil Sis couldn't miss it.

Quickly Dollie whispered, "Pass her spinach to me" to Sallie, who whispered it to the next girl, and the next and the next all the way down until it reached Lil Sis. The girls took action. As the Clacker passed, Lil Sis pushed her spinach onto her neighbor's plate. That neighbor passed it down the line and so on. But each girl not only pushed Lil Sis's spinach onto her plate, she put her own as well. Even Jessa smiled crookedly and heaved her spinach onto Dollie's plate.

Now, the Society stretched food far, and what it considered a serving was half of what a child living in a home with a lowercase *h* would face. But to Dollie, the pile of spinach on her plate was a verifiable mountain. People died scaling such heights.

"Hurry," Sallie whispered as the Clacker moved toward them. "We're all going to get it if you don't—"

But Sallie didn't have to tell her twice. If the Clacker saw the spinach mountain, they'd all be toast. None of them would be watching a real Disney movie.

Dollie closed her eyes and tucked in, not even bothering with a fork. She leaned forward and ate the way the youngest girls worked through their spaghetti the night before, with bulldozer fingers. Green juice dripped down her chin and onto her dress. Sallie's napkin darted to wipe it up.

Clack. Clack. Clack.

The spinach solidified in Dollie's mouth. Working the clump into chewable pieces, she forced it into her belly.

"Keep going! Keep going!" Sallie whispered.

No one else spoke. Every one of the dozen girls turned toward Dollie. None of them moved. None of them breathed. Lil Sis leaned forward, her corkscrew curls swinging. Her face paled and then turned nearly as green as Dollie's spinach mountain.

Clack.

The Clacker paused behind Dollie, who still had a giant serving in front of her despite the enormous amount already in her belly. Dollie scooped a forkful of spinach and then quickly added another and another to her mouth.

The Clacker didn't move. The bench under Dollie shifted as the girls turned away from her and tilted their faces to their own plates. Dollie swallowed. Her stomach rumbled. She risked a glance at the Clacker. This one was new—younger than Mother. The Clacker's mouth twitched. "How is your spinach?"

"It could use a little salt, ma'am." Dollie swallowed.

Next to her Sallie snorted. The Clacker covered her mouth with her hand as giggles erupted down the row. Laughter lit up girl to girl until the whole room glowed. It warmed even Jessa, who reached over Sallie and took half the spinach back.

That's when Madame Brick peeked into the room. She banged her wooden cane onto the polished tiled floor three times. "Whatever is going on in here?" Madame Brick might've been a feeble old woman, but her voice was not. Her voice snuffed that laughter right down to smokeless wick.

The girls faced their plates, heads down.

"We were discussing the merits of seasoning," the Clacker responded coolly. The edge of her gray wool dress brushed against Dollie's back.

"Miss Winters," Madame Brick snapped, "remember your place. You are no longer a resident of the Society for Friendless Children. You are an employee."

The Clacker—Miss Winters—raised her chin. "Oh, I remember."

Next to Dollie, Sallie's mouth popped open. Dollie's eyes widened into huge circles. *Miss Winters was an orphan too?*

Much later that night, Lil Sis once again crawled into Dollie's bed.

This time, Lil Sis wrapped her arms around Dollie's back, smooshing in until Dollie felt her cold little nose against the base of her neck. Dollie sighed but didn't shake her sister away. "Did you like the movie?" she asked instead.

Lil Sis ran a finger along Dollie's ear. "Yes." She sighed. "Silly, though. The puppet didn't need to tell the truth to be real. He always was real, even when he wasn't being true."

Chapter Twelve

As we pulled up to the school, Raymond's mouth screwed tight with the effort of swallowing back what he wanted to say.

"It's funny because they laughed, and she ate all the spinach," I explained.

"Because she had to," Raymond whispered.

"Well, she liked spinach, so it all worked out." I crossed my arms and slumped back into the bus bench. "Listen, about your road trip—"

"No one likes *that much* spinach," Raymond interrupted. I stepped into the aisle and let him go ahead of me, waiting until he was in front with his back turned before yanking my backpack out from where I had shoved it. In the time it took for me to tell that story, my bag had grown roots and now was stubborn as a turnip about giving up its new home wedged under the bus seat. Sara, the only other person still on the bus, sighed and stepped out into the aisle. She helped me yank it out.

"Thanks!" I told her.

Sara pushed her turquoise hair out of her face and nodded. "I'm actually going to miss hearing your stories the next couple of weeks," she said.

I thought about telling her I'd be right with her, but then came to my senses. This was going to be a secret mission. No way would Mama, Daddy, or Mr. Crickett give permission for me to stow away with them. But maybe they'd forgive me? Instead I focused on another thought. "You heard me? All the way in the back of the bus?"

Sara nodded.

"Is that because you don't see as well? Does that mean your ears work better?"

Sara sighed, her shoulders rising high. "No," she said, her voice sharp. "It's because you're very loud."

She shoved the backpack into my arms and returned to the back of the bus.

I wobbled as I raced down the aisle and off the bus before the driver shifted into gear.

Just as I stepped off the bus, Raymond stopped suddenly and turned around. I bounced off him, nearly falling backward.

"Why do you gotta prove these stories are true, Trixy?" he asked. "Wouldn't it be better just to be like Lil Sis says—figure that being real is just as important as being true?"

"I don't know what you're saying, Raymond Crickett."

He took a big breath. "You already know that Gran was real, always was real, even if the stories she told ain't the whole truth."

I was so boiling mad I wanted to kick Raymond right in his good-for-nothing shin. "You read those stories all wrong," I snarled. "Gran told me the *truth*."

"I think maybe *you* heard the stories wrong." Raymond's mouth twisted in that same way it did the first day I got back on the bus after Gran passed. I hate that sour face. I hate it so much. He cleared his throat. "Maybe if you follow those stories to where they lead, you're going to be sorry. Maybe you would wish you had left them alone."

"Just when I thought you were okay, Raymond, you turn out to be about as useful as high heels on a donkey." A thousand bees couldn't compare to the buzzing in my ears. Maybe I was hearing something no one else could hear. Maybe I was hearing rage.

"I *have* to prove those stories. I have to make Mama hear them. Ever since Gran died, Mama's changed. If she can talk about her, if she can share her stories like I can, maybe she'll stop pushing everything away, running from everything. Maybe she'll go back to normal if we can still talk about Gran." Raymond blinked at me. I took a deep breath, and the bees flew away. "I'm sorry. I shouldn't have called you a fancy ass."

We walked toward the school. Kids streamed out of buses all around us. "You make it hard to be your friend," he said, his voice bitter. "If I hadn't promised . . ."

"Promised?" I echoed, the word bouncing like it was a stone thrown down a canyon. I didn't know if I wanted to hear it land.

Raymond didn't finish his sentence.

Catrina once again awaited my arrival at the top of the school stairs.

She thrust a single sheet of paper at me when I finally reached her. "*This*," she said, "is a *true* story about my *actual* life. It's going to win the story contest this year. Thought you should know."

I shrugged. "We'll see."

Catrina was so furious that her whole body vibrated. She leaned forward, nostrils flaring and eyes bulging. "We *will* see. *You* will see especially. You will see me win."

I took the paper from Catrina's hand. Her story was

about learning how to do a cartwheel so she could join the Pixie cheerleading team. The story ended with this line: *The lesson I learned is that hard work leads to s-u-c-c-e-s-s, just like the cheer I made up for the team.*

I felt like those girls who had watched Dollie conquer Spinach Mountain: I couldn't stop the giggle bubbling from deep inside me, even as Catrina waved her angry arms around more than Madame Brick's cane.

"My story is. Not. Funny, Trixy Mae Williams," Catrina hissed. "Why are you laughing?"

I hiccupped. "It's not funny, it's b-o-r-i-n-g, Catrina. Also, you did not make up that cheer. Pixies have been saying that cheer my whole life."

"*My* story has a lesson." Catrina snatched the paper out of my hands. "Judges love lessons. Your stories—which aren't even about you and most definitely are *not* true—are just a bunch of nonsense."

I took that final step so I could be the same size as Catrina. (Well, not technically, since I was still a little bean and she was tall as a carrot, but it made me feel like I was tall as her.) "My gran's stories are not nonsense. You said it yourself, Catrina. My stories make a difference! Miss Brown is different because of them. So is Miranda Sherman. So is Raymond Crickett. I bet even your mom is different since she read them."

Catrina waved her paper around. "So what if she's talking about your stories? She's a librarian. It's her job. It doesn't change a thing. Rules are rules, and your stories aren't meant for this competition."

I thought about Dollie, being brave and scared all at once as she stood up to Henry, to Madame Brick, to Miss Winters. I thought about the stories I hadn't shared yet, and how much braver still Dollie was going to have to be. "*I* am different because of them too. Brave enough to say you better leave me alone!"

Catrina took a step backward, her chest rising and falling. "And I'm going to be in that contest," I vowed. "Not because I don't want you to win. Not just because you're mean and think you're better than everyone else. No, I'm going to enter the contest because my stories are real *and* true. And if being in that contest means I've got to prove it, then that's what I'm going to do. I'm going to prove it to you, to the judges, and to Mama that Gran told me the truth." I took another step toward her. "I'm a storyteller. I get it natural, just like my gran. And she wants her stories told, so I'm not going to keep them to myself anymore."

Catrina pushed her chin in the air. "Your gran doesn't want her stories told," she said with words that quaked. Her face set in mean lines. "She doesn't want *anything*. Know why? Because she's *dead*, Trixy. She's *gone.* She's never, *ever* coming back. And she doesn't care one bit about her stories *or you* anymore."

And that's when a swarm of bees poured out of me so fast they knocked Catrina Alfonso right down the stairs.

I hadn't seen the people crowded around us while we had yelled back and forth atop those stairs. I hadn't noticed Mrs. Brown rushing toward me from behind Catrina. I hadn't noticed anything at all, including my very own hands rising and giving her a shove.

All I noticed was her falling backward, and how it seemed to happen much too fast. If it were a movie, it would've been slow motion, with time for me to offer a drawn-out *"Noooooooo!"* If it were a movie, I would've had time to grasp the top of her dress and pull her back.

But it was real life, so that meant Catrina Alfonso fell backward, flailing, and then her back bumped against the handrail a couple of steps down from where we stood before Mrs. Brown could grab and steady her.

All around us, people screamed. Miranda Sherman peed her pants (which actually isn't all that unusual; she has a fragile bladder). Catrina sucked in all the air in the entire state. Everything seemed to rush toward her as she did, our bodies stretching like putty. And then, *wham.* She let loose all that air in one walloping scream that blew us back to proper proportions.

"Where does it hurt?" Mrs. Brown asked Catrina.

But Catrina kept right on screaming. She raised one hand and pointed a finger at me. The scream morphed into my name.

Catrina pulled in a body-stretching gulp of air. "She *pushed* me!"

I shook my head. Then nodded. Mrs. Brown's eyes narrowed.

Miranda Sherman ran inside. "I'll get the nurse!" she shouted. "I need to change anyway!"

"Everyone else, get to class," Mrs. Brown ordered. "Not you, Trixy," she said as I turned around. "*You* need to go to the principal's office. I will meet you there shortly."

Catrina smiled then, a big smile that stretched from ear to ear.

"You seem to be feeling better," Mrs. Brown noted.

Instantly Catrina whimpered and limped up the stairs, though her mouth twitched as she passed by me.

Daddy picked me up after the principal got all of his hollering out of his system.

The office ladies had tried again and again to reach Mama. If she was out running, she'd be miles away, probably without any reception. So, when Daddy showed, it was in his work blues, the quarry dust clinging to his hair and his beard. He rushed toward me so fast that Principal Winchester stepped in front of me. "Now, I know we're all concerned about this situation but—"

Daddy didn't pause, just stepped around him and gathered me, crushing me against him in a hug. "What happened, Trixy Mae?" he said right in my ear, tickling me with his beard.

Until that moment, I had been holding myself together just fine. But with Daddy's arms around me, I splintered and crumbled. "I pushed her," I finally managed to choke out. "I didn't mean to, but she was saying the most awful things about me, about Gran, and I forgot all about the stairs, Daddy, honest I did." I pulled in a breath and felt the bits of me settle back together.

Daddy dropped his arms and looked me square in the face. He was so close I could see a mini Trixy inside his dark eyes. I waited for him to tell me it was okay, that I didn't have to worry, that he'd make everything better. He shook his head instead. "Trixy," he said in his big booming voice, "what you did was wrong. You *hurt* that girl."

His words scalded my face. I wiped them away. "I think she's faking most of it." *Wasn't he even going to ask me what she had said?*

"If someone wrongs you, you don't get to wrong them back," Daddy said. "Imagine if that's how the world ran. We'd be nothing but hurt." He turned to Principal Winchester. "How do we make this right?"

Principal Winchester was a short, thin man with hair that only grew in a ring from ear to ear. At one point during the past hour, I thought maybe his hair had jumped right off his head to escape hearing him say, "And how do you *feel about that*?" one more time. He rocked back on his heels. "Well, Trixy and I had a nice discussion. And I did get an e-mail from Mrs. Alfonso just now, assuring me that Catrina appears to be doing fine."

Daddy and I both exhaled.

"But," Principal Winchester continued, "we have a strict school policy on school fights. And that's why I'm going to have to suspend Trixy for a week."

Daddy and I both inhaled. "A *week*?" we said together.

Principal Winchester nodded.

"Trixy can't go to school for a full week?" Daddy asked.

There was a part of me, a very, very small part no bigger than my littlest freckle, that thought . . . well, I'd rather not admit to such things.

"Go on back to my classroom and gather your belongings," Mrs. Brown said from her corner. To Daddy, she added, "I'll make sure to send home materials."

Back in the quiet classroom—everyone else was at music class—I pulled my new stories out of my backpack. I slipped them to the bottom of the stack of tests Mrs. Brown had yet to grade on her desk. Hopefully she wouldn't find them for days. On top was a note I had written last night: *I figured I'd get a head start on the makeup work I'm going to have to do when I get back.*

Last week, Mrs. Brown had taught us a new word. *Serendipitous.* She told us it meant a convenient accident, like when you put on a pair of pants and find five dollars in the pocket on a day you forgot to pack lunch. Or when you push Catrina Alfonso down the stairs and get suspended for a week just before you were planning to run away with Raymond Crickett.

Chapter Thirteen

Daddy didn't talk as we drove home in his pickup truck.

He steered with his left hand on the wheel, the right arm resting on the console between us. I saw his hand, relaxed with his thumb resting against his forefinger, and wanted to slip my own hand inside it. But I didn't.

He already was disappointed in me. When he found out what I had planned, that would be so much worse.

He wouldn't understand it at all, just like I knew he didn't understand why I had pushed Catrina.

For Daddy, things were right, or they were wrong.

But sometimes things were both.

Pushing Catrina wasn't both—I knew that was flat-out wrong.

I knew running away was wrong too. Yet proving Gran's stories was *right.* And not because of some silly contest. Not because it might make my ears stop buzzing like a beehive full of secret stories either. It was because Gran had *wanted* to go on that trip. She had wanted to show me that her stories had been true. Everyone's stories should be heard.

Gran should've had more time to tell hers.

Most of all, I *had* to prove the stories so Mama would believe in them. Then maybe she'd start believing me too, that talking about Gran was good, that it was okay to still need her. Maybe Mama would pause, listen to them, listen to *me*, and I wouldn't feel so lonely, as though I was losing them both.

When we pulled into the driveway, Mama was running down the road toward home in her sweatpants and a sweatshirt, despite it being nearly eighty-five degrees outside. Daddy saw her heading toward us as he shifted the car into park. He sighed. For a moment, I thought he might cry. He does that sometimes. At Gran's funeral, his face was chapped with tears. But this time, he didn't. He said, "All right, Trix. Go on inside."

"Aren't you going to come?"

Daddy shook his head, eyes still on Mama. "No, I've already missed an hour of work because of this. Now get on."

"But what am I going to tell Mama?"

Daddy patted me on the head. "You've gotta own up to the truth. That's part of your punishment."

"What are you doing here?" asked Mama, huffing as she checked the little watch on her bony wrist. She was always checking that watch, but never for the time. It tracked her steps. If the number wasn't high enough before she went to bed, she would march in place until it was. "Did Daddy drop you off?"

"Why didn't you check your phone?" I said, suddenly angry instead of sorry.

Mama put her hands on her hips. "I don't look at my phone on runs. I keep it on silent. It's too much of a distraction."

"But I needed you." I put my hands on my hips too.

Mama bent her leg to stretch the muscles. "Please, enough with the dramatics. Just tell me what's going on."

"I got suspended." When Mama gasped, I added, "Just for a week, though!"

"Suspended! For a week! What did you do, Trixy Mae?"

"My hands accidentally pushed Catrina down the stairs."

Mama wobbled a bit.

"She's not really hurt or anything."

Mama's chest rose and fell. Her mouth flopped open

and her eyes closed like a doll I used to have when I was smaller.

"It's just a week," I whispered.

And then Mama collapsed.

"Mama! *Mama!*" I screamed. "Please, Mama, wake up!" I hovered over her, my knees on each side of her body and my hands holding her face. "Please, Mama!"

For a second, everything turned black. I saw a flash of light and heard a scream. That second seemed to burst like a bubble, soaking me in fear. I couldn't lose Mama too. What if she didn't wake up? Gran hadn't woken up. "Mama!"

I pressed my ear to her chest, her ribs hard through her sweatshirt. I heard a faint beat. She was alive.

I didn't want to leave her—a silly part of me was sure if I did, she'd disappear—so it took a couple of tries to convince my legs to move. Then I bolted into the house. Inside the door, I fell down on my knees, pushed up, and kept running until I reached the kitchen, where the house phone rested on its cradle. I dialed 9-1-1 while rushing back to Mama. "Help!" I said when the operator answered. "Help me! I think my mama is dying!"

"We're sending help," the operator told me.

She asked me for Daddy's phone number, and it took me a minute to remember the number. "I'm sorry," I hiccupped into the phone. My whole body was shaking so hard that even my teeth chattered. "I don't know what's wrong with me."

"Oh, sweetie. You're scared. But you're okay. Help's on the way."

She stayed on the line with me and asked me to count Mama's breaths. I counted them out loud, over and over, my hand pressed against her chest to feel when it moved up and down. My body never stopped shaking. It seemed to want to run in every direction all at once.

Soon sirens blared in the distance, and there were police and an ambulance at our house in what I knew was just twelve minutes, thanks to the timer on the phone, but also was an entire year. "They're here," I told the lady on the phone.

"You did great, sweetie. I'm proud of you."

One of the emergency workers gently pulled my hand from Mama's and waved something under her nose. He used his knuckles to rub on her chest. Mama's eyelashes fluttered and then she opened them.

"She's alive," I whispered, and for just a second my body stilled, some of that fear seeping away.

"Of course she is," answered the man. He nodded to someone behind him, another person in a white uniform.

"Hey, there," she said to Mama. "My name's Maggie. When did you last eat?"

Mama said she couldn't remember.

"Looks like you were exercising," Maggie said. "How far did you go today?"

"Just a few miles. It wasn't my longest run."

Maggie and the other ambulance helper shared a glance. They raised her onto a bed, and then one of them slipped a needle in the crook of her arm. Mama seemed to fall back asleep. Maggie listened to Mama's heart with a stethoscope. "Strong and steady," she said, and my own heart seemed to settle. Maggie checked a little clip she had put around Mama's pointer finger. "Oxygen level is solid."

The man wheeled Mama toward the ambulance.

"You've been really brave," Maggie said. "Your dad will be here soon."

I didn't feel brave. Just scared and cold and alone. *Mama.* All that shaking knocked loose my tears, and they poured out of me when I spotted dust blowing as Daddy's truck raced too fast toward the house. Daddy jumped out without remembering to turn off the engine and I ran toward him, bawling like a baby. He picked me right up and crushed me to him for the second time that day. Without putting me down, we went over to where they were loading Mama onto the ambulance. "Jenny!" he called. "Jenny, what's going on?"

Maggie put a hand on Daddy's shoulder and spoke

softly, her eyes sliding to mine and back to Daddy's. "I think she's fine. Dehydrated. Didn't eat enough today."

At that, Daddy hiccupped. Tears streamed down his cheeks.

Maggie swallowed and again looked at me. "She's quite thin. We're going to take her to Mercy General. Why don't you meet us there?"

Daddy nodded, and I slid down his side so my feet touched the ground again. I wasn't crying anymore, and my teeth had stopped chattering. Maybe it's possible to feel so much all at once that it seems like you're not feeling anything at all. Like you're hollow.

Peculiar, isn't it, how wanting to cry goes away when you want someone else *not* to cry?

I waited beside Mama's hospital bed for her to wake. Daddy had been in the hall, talking with the doctor.

When he came back in, I sat up straighter. "What is anorexia?"

Daddy blew out all of his air as though I had pricked him with a needle. He was a deflated balloon, about to slide right off the chair. "Trixy, you know better than to eavesdrop."

I didn't say anything. I wished for that hollow feeling to come back. I don't know what was worse—feeling scared like I had back at the house, or whatever was swirling through me now. Something that whispered ugly words. Something that told me this was all my fault.

Daddy rubbed his forehead. "It means she doesn't eat enough. It's bigger than that, but that's the gist of it." He lowered his hands. "Since we lost Gran, and almost lost you, something chipped loose inside her. Your mama, well, she's pretty sick." Daddy's booming voice shook.

My fault. "That's why she passed out?"

Daddy nodded. "She was doing too much, eating too little, and it just got to be more than she could handle."

I nodded, my eyes on Mama. In the hospital gown, there was no mistaking the way her body didn't curve like it used to. Mama had never been a big woman, but she had been softer, rounder. Not anymore. Daddy wasn't the only one who had been trying to ignore it. "I'm sorry," I whispered, and I didn't know whom I was saying it to—Daddy, Mama, or Gran. "It's my fault."

"You stop it, Trixy," Daddy said, and then, before I could even blink, he was kneeling in front of me. His hands were on my cheeks.

My chin wobbled. I tried to push down the ugliness I felt, but I couldn't, not with his eyes locked on mine like that.

"It is *not* your fault!" Daddy was looking at me fiercely. "Why would you think that?"

"'Cause I told her about Catrina." Wouldn't you know it, all those tears I had stored burst loose. "That's when she fell."

Daddy's hands dropped to rest on my shoulders. He tilted his head, as though he couldn't believe what I was saying. "Oh, Trix. She would've fallen regardless."

I had to make Daddy understand. "Because of me." I closed my eyes. "I made Gran have the accident. I was asking her to tell me more stories, and she did. She turned in her seat to look at me. If she hadn't, she would've seen the stop sign. She wouldn't—"

"You listen to me, Trixy Mae," Daddy said, his words so soft but still strong enough to part the swirling feelings inside me. "You and Gran had an accident. A horrible accident. And it was not your fault. It just plain wasn't. There wasn't anything Gran loved more than you. Bad things happen sometimes, and this was a bad thing. But it was not your fault. Do you hear me?"

I nodded, my chin still wobbling and my eyes still closed.

"You look at me, Trixy Mae."

I opened my eyes and all I saw was Daddy staring right back at me.

"None of this is your fault." His jaw tightened. "You're a little girl. What happened is much bigger than you and *not your doing.*" Daddy let go of one of my shoulders to rub at the back of his neck. "I know you love stories. I know your mind likes putting them together. But this"—he glanced toward where Mama slept—"this is part of *her* story. Not yours."

The swirling in my chest settled just a little. I wasn't sure I believed him that this wasn't my fault. But I believed that he didn't think it was so. And I knew that he loved me.

He pulled me close and cradled my head against his heart. *Thump, thump, thump.*

A therapist came in a little later to talk with all three of us. Mama could've asked me to leave the room, but she didn't. Daddy held my hand. The social worker told us that sometimes people's food stops being something that sustains them and becomes something for them to control. Food and exercise turned into something Mama felt like she was able to control when her feelings were too big to manage. Only now, she couldn't control those, either. Mama reached out, but she didn't swat Daddy's arm; she patted it instead. I thought about the swirling fear inside me when she fell, how it made it so I couldn't think or feel anything else. Did Mama feel that way all the time? Was she trying to feel hollow instead?

Would she ever just feel okay?

Almost like she heard the thought, the therapist said, "To get better, we have to reset your brain, Jennifer."

She said Mama should go to a special treatment center where she could talk to therapists and could connect with other people managing eating disorders.

"How long?" Daddy asked the palms of his hands.

Mama didn't say anything, just stared at the ceiling. Her arm slid back to her side.

The clock *tick, tick, ticked* on the far wall. Somehow it was only noon.

"I think we've identified this disease at an early enough stage that we can concentrate on mindset. I recommend a few days of inpatient care for intensive therapy," the counselor said.

"What does *inpatient* mean?" I asked. My voice was so soft I didn't think anyone would hear, but the counselor smiled at me.

"It means she'll spend the night at the treatment center."

I nodded, but I was still confused.

"Once Jennifer is feeling stronger, we'll transition to daily out-patient therapeutic care. Don't misunderstand, out-patient care will be significant—at least eight hours, every day. This is a process, one that we'll adjust depending on the goals you meet. After several weeks of daylong therapy, we might be able to scale back to group sessions."

I tried to imagine our house without Mama, even if it was just for the few days she'd be at a treatment center. My heart thumped. What if she didn't come back?

Mama rolled onto her side. "Is this necessary?" she asked the wall.

And then I remembered something else—I was suspended. If I didn't hitch a ride out of town with the Cricketts, Daddy would have to take the time off work just to stay home with me now that Mama was being sent away. How much trouble would he get into with his boss? I closed my eyes. *Please, Gran,* I thought as hard as I could. *Please let me get home in time to leave with Raymond tonight.*

A small part of me whispered that I just wanted to run away because I didn't want to think about Mama being sick. That I didn't want to miss her in a house already emptied of Gran. That I'd be making an ugly situation worse by running away in the middle of it. But I told that part to hush up. I might not be able to make Mama better, but I could get out of town before I made things worse.

The counselor and Daddy worked on the details of Mama's care. She would be transferred as soon as possible. Daddy followed the counselor into the hallway.

"I feel like a puppet," Mama muttered, and I knew it wasn't to me. "Everyone else pulling the strings."

I thought about crawling into the bed with Mama, my arms around her the way Lil Sis had curled against Dollie so long ago, but I stayed put. I thought about how Mama used to laugh, her head falling back. I thought about how when Gran was alive, we all revolved around Mama. She was the one who directed when we ate, where we went, what I wore, which chores we each had to do. I thought about how Gran would pass by her, stopping to kiss the top of Mama's head, how Mama would smile. I thought about that terrible day, how when I woke up, Mama's face was buried in my hair.

My mind fluttered from thought to thought, not able to stay put in one spot long enough to solve any of the questions in my head. Not even long enough for me to understand what I was feeling.

"Are you really suspended?" Mama whispered. "I think I remember you saying you were suspended."

I nodded without thinking; Mama still was facing the wall. Her shoulder blades looked like too-short wings popping out from her back. "Yes," I said.

"Catrina must've made you pretty mad."

Bitterness swelled through me, thinking of what she had said, and the way her face had twisted while those barbed words pushed through her mouth. And then I thought about the way Mama had fallen over, just because she wouldn't eat. Mama not waking up when I screamed her name. My mind whirled, going back further to other times I needed her and she wasn't there. Or if she was, she wasn't really. Not fully.

I needed her. *I* hurt too. *My* feelings were too big for me too. Why hadn't she taken care of herself? I already lost Gran; why did she let herself fade away too? "I've been madder."

The words were bricks, building a thick wall between me and Mama. "Was it about Gran?" Mama asked. "Whatever Catrina said, I mean."

I didn't answer.

Mama nodded as though I had. "I wish you'd stop thinking about those stories, Trixy. Listen to reason. Mrs. Brown told me about one of them—something improbable about a bakery. If they were true, where's Lil Sis? Not once did Gran mention I had an aunt. Not *once.* She was an orphan, Trixy, never had family."

"Gran told me she lost her. She . . . she died, I guess. I found a picture, you know. It showed all the kids at the orphanage. And one of them held the hand of another one. I think it was Gran and Lil Sis."

Mama sighed. "It could've been anyone." She rolled toward me, breaking down that wall between us and looking at me with red eyes. "Here's what I think. She was a horribly lonely child. She invented an imaginary friend so she'd never be alone."

"Lil Sis was real. She was *real*! Gran wouldn't make up something like that. I'll find out the truth and prove it to you. She wants me to do it; that's why my ears have been buzzing. It's Gran, pushing me to prove it to you and everyone else!"

"Your ears have nothing to do with Gran, Trixy! You just have water in them or you listen to music too loud or have an allergy or something. They'll get back to normal soon and—"

"No!" I shouted, too loudly because a nurse paused in the hall. Mama waved and she kept going. "No," I repeated, softer but still loudly. "It's magic, some sort of magic Gran created so I can hear—"

This time Mama was the one who shouted. "You're too old to believe in magic!" She sat upright in the bed and pointed as she yelled. "There's no such thing as magic and those fairy tales she spun you are simply not true. Face it, Trixy, she is *gone.* And no matter how badly you want her to be here, no matter what you wish you could tell her or hear her say back, you *can't.* You can't!"

"Stop it!" I yelled, and for a moment, I was on top of the steps about to shove Catrina once more. "You don't know anything!"

"I do, Trixy," Mama hollered right back. "I do know! You need to push all of those stories away and move on!"

"Like you? No!" My hands curled into fists. "I hate you! I hate you!"

I opened my mouth, wanting to swallow back the words, but it was too late.

Mama blinked and tears dropped down her cheek. "I know you don't mean that."

I stared down at my shoes.

"To you, she was a wonderful grandmother. She was kind to me, she was there for me, she loved me, but she kept so much of her life bottled and tucked away. So much she'd never tell me. Being responsible for me, I think she wasn't ready for the enormity of it. Again and again, she told me I was all she had. I spent most of my childhood terrified something would happen to her and I wouldn't have anyone at all."

"You have me. You have Daddy," I said. "And you're scaring *me*."

Mama slumped in the bed. "My mother, she knew how to hold sadness. She spent most of her life being lonely. Loneliness can make people think strange things, tell themselves stories that aren't real. It can make them do things they—"

"This isn't about *you*," I growled.

Mama's face turned red as a slap. After a long pause, she said, "Trixy, I . . ."

"I'll prove it to you," I told her. "I'll prove that her stories are true and worth sharing." I didn't wait to hear what she said next. I pushed back my chair and stomped from the room.

Chapter Fourteen

Mama was going to be transferred to Pondview Treatment Center, which was in the next town over. It was a place for adults with eating disorders. The counselor and doctor acted like it was a surprise birthday party that it had an open spot.

"You're so lucky they have a bed for her," the counselor said with a toothy smile. "There is almost always a waiting list there!"

Daddy had squeezed my hand then, and I knew we were thinking the same thing—other families, just like ours. Other mamas, just like mine.

The two of us went home to gather some things she would need.

"She'll live there for a week at most, and then come home," Daddy told me. He was folding Mama's shirts and putting them into a suitcase. "Things will be different then."

Things already were different. I tucked Mama's toothbrush and hairbrush into the front of the suitcase.

Days or years had passed since I had called the ambulance, though the clock told me it was just a few hours.

"Well, one thing's for certain true," I said into the silence between us once Daddy zipped the bag. He didn't prompt me to continue, so I went on ahead. "It's a really good thing I pushed Catrina down those stairs."

For a moment, Daddy didn't move. "And how do you figure that?" he finally asked. The ringing in his ears must've been extra loud because his whole body seemed to vibrate.

"'Cause that meant I was home when Mama fell," I explained.

Daddy didn't say anything else, not even when we sat together at the dining room table. I suppose he was as mixed up as I was with time, considering it was just four o'clock in the afternoon, yet he made dinner. He was even confused about what meal we were having. Scrambled eggs, toast with butter, pancakes, and apple slices pan fried with cinnamon.

After we ate, Daddy rubbed at his beard with his hand.

"I'm going to go back to the hospital. I'll give Mrs. Murphy next door a call, and she'll stay with you until I get home."

"Can I go to Raymond's instead?" I asked. "I can walk there. I'd . . ." Guilt slithered inside me. "I'd really like to be with a friend," I finished, and then held my breath. If he remembered that the Cricketts were leaving for their road trip tonight, my plan would be squashed.

Daddy watched my face. I wondered what he saw. His mouth twitched and he seemed to nod to himself. "You shouldn't be hanging out with a friend the day you get suspended from school, but these are special circumstances. I'm not sure when I can pick you up from the Cricketts. Probably not till past Raymond's bedtime."

"I'll come home." I straightened my back. "I'll tuck myself in. I'm big enough for that."

Daddy looked at me with sad eyes. "You sure? Mrs. Murphy could come over—"

"I'll be fine! I'll call her if I need her." I cleared our plates so I wouldn't have to look at Daddy while I pushed my words past that slime monster slithering around my throat. I felt like I was choking.

"I can do hard things, Dad," I said.

"Dad?" he echoed. He swallowed; I saw the bump in his throat bob, and I wondered what his words were working past. He stared down at the vinyl tablecloth.

"Daddy," I said instead.

"I know you can, Trixy. You proved that today, didn't you?"

And I knew he wasn't talking about pushing Catrina. He was talking about calling for help.

That slime monster grew tentacles and squeezed my chest.

What I was planning to do was going to hurt him. Hopefully Mama wouldn't know about it; she'd be safe and sound at that center. At the same time, I could prove Gran's stories. And *that* might help Mama too. A mean little part of me, a part I didn't like at all, hissed that running away might show Mama how much about me she didn't know, how much she missed by paying all her attention to staying hollow inside and not to me. I told that bit of me to stop being so ugly.

Maybe Daddy wouldn't tell Mama I ran away at all. Maybe when she was back home, we'd show her proof of Gran's stories, and he'd tousle my hair and say, "You gave me a scare, Trix, but I understand." Maybe he'd even thank me for making this whole thing easier by leaving so he could go to work while Mama was in treatment.

I'm good at telling myself lies.

I thought about Mama in that hospital bed, about what she said, how she didn't know Gran, not the way I did, the way she never would. I thought about what Gran said about stories, about how the wrong ears could bend the way they settle. I had always thought that meant her stories were just for me. But maybe she hadn't been able to tell them to Mama. Maybe she knew someday I could. I thought about what it meant to be brave, what it meant to be wrong. I thought about Dollie, and all she did for Lil Sis, and how Mama didn't even believe she was real.

This is the truth.

Gran loves me. She *still* loves me, no matter what Catrina says.

Her stories are real.

She wants them to be told.

And this also is the truth: What I planned to do was going to make everything harder for everyone, even me. Especially me.

After Daddy's truck turned down the driveway and out of sight, I bunched the pillows and blankets on my bed to look like I was asleep.

Then I wrote Daddy a note. *I know you're going to be mad at me, but I have to prove Gran's stories are true. I need to know they're real, and I know you and Mama have other stuff to deal with right now, so I'm going to do it on my own. I'll be safe, and I'll be back soon. Don't tell Mama.* I slipped it under the blankets, on top of a stack of every story I had written, including the ones I had left with Mrs. Brown earlier today.

Something happened as I had printed those stories, as I looked down at the straight rows of words. The stack was heavy in my hands. The way Gran had told them to me, they weren't sad. They were just her stories, about her life, and they just *were*. But now? Seeing them and holding them in my hands, moving them from what she told me to what I wrote, they changed. Instead of just hearing them, I *felt* them. Maybe that was another reason why Gran hadn't wanted to share her stories before now. Maybe she knew that made them true for someone else in a way they weren't for her. Maybe she knew I'd want to know more, that I'd *have* to find out more, once they were shared.

With my backpack full of clothes, I headed to Raymond's house.

Chapter Fifteen

That Raymond Crickett is smart.

Sure, it took him a moment to realize I for sure did intend to run away with him on his family's road trip. We whisper-yelled a bit and both did some foot stomping. Maybe I even blubbered a little about Mama being sent away. But once he accepted that I wasn't staying behind, he got to work.

First thing he did was guard the front door so I could run inside to use the bathroom.

Second, while Mr. Crickett went through the house, checking locks and making sure taps were off, Raymond told Sara he was pretty sure she had left her headphones on her bed. Sara had sighed but had gotten out of the front seat to go check. Within seconds, Raymond cleared out a space under the backseat of the truck for me. I lay flat on my back under the bench seat, and Raymond stacked bags in front of me.

Third, he tucked a blanket around me and handed me a pillow. Fourth, he made sure one of those bags in front of me was full of snacks. “Dad doesn’t stop much,” he whispered, even though his father still was in the house. I ate one of those granola bars right away, rolling onto my side so I didn’t choke. Raymond told me that they’d probably drive all night, getting to Little Bass in the early morning.

I sucked in my breath when the driver’s side door of the pickup truck opened and Mr. Crickett slid in. A minute later, Sara got into the passenger seat and slammed the door, headphones in her ears. None of them said a word as Mr. Crickett shifted into drive and the truck rumbled down the gravel driveway.

After a few seconds, I let out that breath. The sound of the road was loud against my ear, and the metal underneath me was cold. I already was panicky from sneaking away, so my usual heart hammering over being in a car just mingled on in. I mentally thanked Raymond for the blanket and pillow. If I wiggled a little, I could curl my legs. Good thing I was tiny as a bean.

I closed my eyes, picturing the road unfolding in front

of us. Now Mr. Crickett was turning left out of his driveway and onto the main road. He'd be passing the cornfields now. The headlights would turn the barn bright red in the distance. Next he'd pass the edge of my yard, and now, probably my little yellow house with the empty church pew swing. Mr. Crickett's truck was rumbling again, gathering speed, which meant even if I hadn't been squashed under the seat and was instead sitting upright, I'd probably only see a flash of white stone as we passed the plot where Gran was buried.

I kept on picturing the roads of town all the way until we reached the highway, where I knew we'd pass the huge brick hospital building. Somewhere in there, Mama lay on a hospital bed, getting ready to be transferred to a Home where she would learn how to feed her sadness.

Somewhere in there, my dad was sitting with his big hands covering his beard.

Strange, isn't it, how I never felt lonelier than I did in that moment, even knowing that Mama and Daddy both carried the same sadness, the same aching weight of losing Gran and who we used to be. Maybe that's the worst part about being sad: it's so ugly and mean that it convinces you that no one else could ever feel it the way you do.

I imagined I could look right through the coils of the seat above me, through the fabric and cushion, through the metal roof of the truck and right up to the stars. I saw one of them twinkling harder than all the others.

I'm sorry, I whispered instead of wished, and I didn't know if it was to Gran or to Daddy. *I'm sorry, but I have to do this.*

Chapter Sixteen

Mr. Crickett and Sara spoke in such low tones back and forth that I couldn't make out much of what they said.

"Most of the band won't arrive until tomorrow," he told her. "I'm going to catch up on sleep when we get to the hotel, so you and Raymond will need to occupy yourselves."

Sara groaned. "Do I *have* to take Raymond to the diner? Can't he go by himself?"

The seat above me creaked as Raymond leaned forward. "Yeah, I can totally go by myself. No problem. I'll be totally alone without anyone and that would be fine."

I pushed farther back in my seat as Sara twisted around. "Could you be any more dramatic?"

"Sara," Mr. Crickett said, "part of why I bring you guys

along on this trip is so that you and Raymond spend time with each other."

She snorted. "And there's the fact that we don't have anyone else."

Mr. Crickett shifted in his seat. "That's not true. I'm sure Trixy's fam—"

"Something's off there," Sara cut in. "Have you seen her mom lately? She's constant—"

Raymond started humming super loudly, blocking out whatever Sara was about to say. Mr. Crickett murmured something too low for me to hear.

Raymond shifted a lot over top of me. I tried to stay still and not think about how cold I was under the bench. Another thought had burst into my mind, and I worked on shoving it back out. That thought was about how I wasn't wearing a seat belt.

My mouth flooded with a metallic taste.

I squeezed my eyes shut as though the image I was seeing was outside rather than in. Gran turning backward in her seat to touch my face. To tell me her stories were just for me. A moment later, lights blaring all around. The crash. The noise and rush like being flung toward a star.

Don't move. Don't move. Usually when the memory of the accident seeped into my mind, I could sidestep it by doing something else—talking to the kids around me (which is what got me into such a pickle with Mrs. Brown at the beginning of the year) or turning up music super loud in my room. But now I just had to lie here.

My heart ping-ponged around the basket of my rib cage, boinging from side to side, up and down. Faster and faster and faster. Soon it was going to burst right through, out of my throat and into this truck. I pulled the bag Raymond had packed in front of me closer, grabbing a bottle of water from it, hoping I could swallow down my heart.

And that's when Mr. Crickett turned on the radio. An old blues singer with a husky voice crooned. I was surprised; I had thought for sure Mr. Crickett would only listen to folk music.

I peeked from under the seat to see Mr. Crickett drumming his fingers on the wheel. Raymond hummed along. Soon Sara slipped her headphones from her ears and picked up the melody. And then they all were singing—Mr. Crickett's deep, rich voice; Raymond's surprisingly light and happy voice; Sara's full, smooth tone—about how they'd be together rain or shine. Sara could *sing*. I had heard her voice before, when Gran and I would go to their porch on our nightly walks, but she must've been perfecting her skills. I had shivers up and down my arms.

My heart bounced to the beat, and then finally back to its regular rhythm. Now that it had calmed, I was more tired than I had ever been in my life. I closed my eyes.

I don't know how much time passed before I opened them again. In the seat above me, Raymond also must've been asleep. His arm was twisted under him as he lay on his side, the fingertips slipping between the seat and the door. If I stretched out, I could touch them. Something about that made me feel better. I closed my eyes again.

Hours later, the truck rumbled to a stop. A good thing about being so small is that I had space to stretch after my long rest. Mr. Crickett told Raymond and Sara he'd check in at the hotel, and that they could wait in the truck, but Sara told him she had to use the bathroom in the lobby. As she got out of the cab, she unsnapped a folded-up white cane, sweeping it back and forth in front of her as she walked into the building behind her dad.

I scrambled out from under the seat.

"Does your sister usually use a cane?" I asked.

Raymond blinked like he couldn't understand my question. "I'm having second thoughts about this, Trixy. You're going to get in big trouble. I'm going to get in big trouble. This whole thing is—"

"Big trouble," I finished for him in a whisper. "I know, but it's too late now. Will Sara see me if I go use the bathroom too?"

"Yes, Sara will see you!" Raymond snapped. "What are you thinking?"

"Well, she's using a cane. I thought maybe she—"

"Became totally blind since we left school this afternoon, and we just decided to go for a road trip anyway?" Raymond's voice was high and thin, his eyes bulging.

I shrugged.

Raymond pulled in a big breath. "Sara has low vision; you know that. She has enough sight to see a lot of things, just not everything. Like she doesn't see the ground well when she's walking. So, when it's super bright, or getting dark, or she's tired, or we're somewhere new, she uses the cane."

"Oh." I slumped backward to enjoy the feeling of my back against a chair. "So, she *would* see me in the bathroom. I'll wait until you're all in your room and then go in."

"You're going to sleep in the truck?" he asked. "We did *not* think this through."

"It'll be fine," I told him. "Maybe I'll find an empty room in the hotel or something."

"Oh, my stars," Raymond said. "You're going to get kidnapped. You're going to get kidnapped and I'm going to have to track you down and get you back, and you know what, Trixy? I do *not* have a certain set of skills like that movie guy. I don't even know how to tie my shoes without making bunny ears. We're in so much trouble. *So* much trouble."

Raymond sighed again. His sister was right; he was dramatic. After a moment, he said, "She's standing with Dad at the front desk. Now's your chance!"

It was easy as pie to walk into the hotel, right behind Mr. Crickett and Sara, use the bathroom, and brush my teeth. But then I didn't know what to do. I couldn't go back to the truck; Mr. Crickett was unloading it. And I couldn't exactly go to their hotel room.

I peeked from the lobby doors into the parking lot. Day was just breaking, making the sky look like cotton candy. Mr. Crickett stretched and yawned as he pulled bags from the truck, handing one to Sara. His cell phone rang, and he pulled it from his back pocket. He stepped away a few yards and cupped his hand over his free ear to block the nearby highway noise. Sara trailed behind him.

This was my chance! I darted toward Raymond, who stood on the far side of the truck. He jumped like a tick when I poked his shoulder. "Get down! Get down!" he cried, even though I was literally crouched down.

Mr. Crickett took a few more steps away, his back toward us. Raymond opened the door of the truck. "Hurry," he whispered. "Get back inside. I'll come let you out when

Dad's asleep. Dad will sleep for a couple of hours, and that's when I usually go to that diner."

"But you'll go with me to the orphanage?" I pressed. He winced but nodded. "Figure out a way to lose Sara, okay?"

"So much trouble," Raymond whined, his face flushing. He took a big breath and nodded. "I promised."

"Promised what?" I asked. He had hinted something similar before.

But before he could answer, Raymond pointed to the back of the truck. "Hurry! Hurry! He's coming back."

Quick as a clap, I bounced into the truck and slid under the backseat. Raymond shut the door and pressed his back against it.

But a second later, the door flew open, and a big tattooed hand reached under the seat, grabbing me by the elbow and yanking me out.

"Just what in heaven do you think you're doing?" boomed a powerful voice.

"Told you," Sara said, her voice bored.

Chapter Seventeen

I squeezed shut my eyes as Mr. Crickett yanked me from my hiding place under the seat of the truck. His voice boomed, "Raymond Crickett, why is this little girl stowed away in our truck?"

I hopped out to stand in front of Raymond, my heart pounding nearly out of my chest. "It's not his fault! I was sneaky."

Mr. Crickett puffed air from his cheeks. He tugged on his beard. "Trixy Mae. It's been a while since I've seen you last."

"Not since Gran died," I said. It was getting easier to say her name. I barely felt the pinch in my chest and buzz in my ears.

Mr. Crickett shook his head like he was clearing it, and then pointed at Raymond. "Ain't no way I'm going to believe you didn't know about this," he said. "And ain't no way you are getting out of this without some sort of consequence." He rubbed at his eyes. "But I've been driving for six hours straight, and I've got to meet up with the band for a show this afternoon."

"I can explain," I said, my voice shaken by my ping-ponging heart.

Mr. Crickett raised one finger. "I don't want to hear it. Not yet." He pulled his phone out of his back pocket, pressed a button, and said, "Yeah, man. You were right. I've got her." He thrust the phone toward me.

When I didn't take it, he held it next to my ear.

"Trixy?" Daddy asked on the other line. There was something horrible about how his voice was the softest I'd ever heard it, yet it blasted through me. "Trixy, how could you do this?"

I tried to explain, but none of my words made sense to him.

"I have to prove Gran's stories are true," I said into the phone, now holding it myself and pressing it hard enough against my ear that it felt like Daddy was right next to me.

"Why, Trixy?" Daddy's voice went out and back and I knew he was shaking his head. "Don't you think we have enough going on right now? When your mama finds out—"

"Don't tell her!" I yelped. "You don't have to tell her. I'll be back before she's out of the treatment cent—"

Mr. Crickett's and Raymond's eyes shot to each other and then to the ground. Mr. Crickett winced, and they both half turned away from me as though giving us privacy. Sara didn't turn, though. She inched a little closer.

"Your mama and I don't keep secrets from each other," Daddy said. But the words were hollow. Mama *did* keep secrets. She hadn't told either of us that she was fading away faster than a September dandelion. "If this is about that contest—that scholarship—it's not that big of a deal, Trixy. It don't matter."

"It *does* matter. It matters to me, and it's more than the contest. You won't believe me," I said, and now anger made my voice shake. "Gran *wants* me to do this. I know it, Daddy. Mama needs me to do it. My ears . . ."

"*That's* what this is about? Your silly *ears*? Trixy, it's a coincidence. That ringing will go away or you'll get accustomed to it."

Even though Daddy couldn't see me, I stomped my foot. "No. I have to do this." I raised my chin Dollie high, and my voice was steady when I finished. "I'm sorry you don't understand. I'm sorry I can't explain it. But I have to do this. I can't just forget Gran. I can't. None of us should."

Daddy's voice boomed into the phone. "Do you have any idea how hard you just made everything? There was a delay at that treatment place and your mama can't get a bed until this afternoon. I can't just drop everything and drive to middle of nowhere Tennessee to pick you up! I'm already missing two days' work. I could lose my job, Trixy."

A bird hatched in my chest, cracking free and now fighting with its wings to be set loose. It made my whole body shudder. "I didn't know—"

"'Course you didn't know!" Daddy boomed. "You're a kid, and you ain't got no right to make decisions!"

Sara put her hand on my arm. Mr. Crickett turned and held out his hand for the phone, though Daddy still was yelling. "It's okay," Mr. Crickett whispered, and nodded again to the phone.

I handed it over and sagged back against the truck. Whenever I did something foolish, Daddy was the one who hugged me close and told me how to right the wrongs I created. Would I ever be able to make him understand why I ran away? Why I *had* to do this? Something rustled inside me, something that whispered that I didn't *have* to do this. That I had *decided* to do it, even knowing it would hurt Daddy. Would he ever forgive me? Raymond stood on one side of me, Sara on the other. Neither of them lied that it would all be okay.

As Mr. Crickett took a few steps away, I still heard Daddy yelling. Daddy never yelled, not on purpose like that, not to me. Mr. Crickett cleared his throat. "Listen, Ern," he said. "Truth is, this whole thing could help us both out. Sounds like you've got a lot going on. I've got to concentrate on these shows, which leaves Raymond on his own most of the day. Plus, Sara could use some girl time. She'll watch over them while I'm practicing. It'll be good for them to spend time with a friend. How 'bout you let Trixy stick with us the next few days? We could meet up on Saturday. I'll be near Nashville by then."

The booming on the other end stopped for a few seconds, then started back up again. Raymond leaned into my side.

"Yeah," Mr. Crickett said. "Ern, I haven't forgotten how you and Jenny were there for me when . . . well, you know, when Raymond's mom packed up. I don't know what was going on with you—"

Whatever Daddy was telling him made Mr. Crickett wince again. "This ain't nothing," he said. "We got you."

Mr. Crickett, his back still to us, lowered his arm. For a moment, he looked up at the brightening sky. Raymond and I followed his gaze, though Sara just looked straight ahead. Even in the early morning sky, a star twinkled. All of us seemed to pull in air, our shoulders rising and falling at the same time. Mr. Crickett rubbed at the back of his neck with the hand not holding the phone. He seemed to be trying but not quite succeeding at smiling at me. He held out the phone toward me again.

I took it. “Daddy?”

For a moment, he just breathed into the phone. “You listen to Mr. Crickett,” he boomed. “I don’t want to hear ’bout you being any trouble. Got it?”

“Yes. I promise,” I whispered. He sounded sad. Maybe I had gotten used to sad, because it didn’t scare me nearly as much as anger. “Thank you, Daddy.”

A brittle laugh rumbled through the phone. “Don’t thank me, Trix. You’re in a heap of trouble. But it’ll wait for you.”

Mr. Crickett barely spoke to us as we unloaded the truck and went to the hotel room. There were two double beds in the main room and a tiny living room with a pull-out couch. That’s where Sara and I’d be sleeping that night. Mr. Crickett said to get some rest. Soon the room filled with Mr. Crickett’s soft snores. Next to me, Sara’s chest rose and fell. I lay there, thinking I’d do nothing but stare at the ceiling for hours. But soon I was asleep.

“You snore,” Sara told me when I finally opened my eyes. The light filtering from behind the curtain told me an hour or two had passed. “We’re going to the diner for breakfast while Dad sleeps some more," she whispered.

I tiptoed past Mr. Crickett to use the bathroom, and then Sara held the door open for me and Raymond to leave the room.

Mr. Crickett rolled over and rubbed at his eyes as we left. He pointed at both me and Raymond. "Don't think I don't know the two of you are up to something," he said. "Stay out of trouble."

We didn't talk much as we headed toward the diner. Sara's cane clicked against the sidewalk. People seemed scared of the thin white cane, jumping out of its way. Sara didn't pause for them, just strode ahead. The way people parted for her made it feel like we were being led by a bodyguard, if that bodyguard was a skinny teenage girl with blue hair. At an intersection, she looked both ways but seemed to be listening more for cars than looking.

Daddy being mad at me was going to spell trouble for future Trixy, but right-now Trixy felt light and fresh as sun-dried sheets on the wash line. Not having to hide under that truck seat, not wondering where I'd sleep, not worrying about the moment Daddy found me missing—all of that had my feet nearly skipping. Not Raymond, though. He stomped.

"What's wrong, Raymond?" I asked.

"Ha! What's wrong? What's wrong?" Raymond's arms

flapped at his sides. "Just, you know, the fact that my dad is furious at me. That I lied to him. That pretty soon your dad's going to pick you back up, but *my* dad is going to lay into me all the way through the second part of the tour. Hiding a girl under the seat! What was I thinking? The only thing I like about this whole danged trip is this diner, and you're going to hound me to get going to visit an *orphanage*."

"Wait," Sara snapped. "What?"

"There's just an old orphanage I want to see," I said. "No big deal."

"Uh-huh." Sara turned to face me. She pointed to her eyes with the hand not holding the cane. "See how my eyes are moving back and forth? That's called nystagmus. I was born with it, and I can't control it. But just so you know, if I were capable of rolling my eyes, I'd be doing that right now."

"Well, I *am*," Raymond said. "I *am* rolling my eyes." In fact, he rolled his whole head.

"Oh, Raymond," I said. "You're so dramatic."

"Me?" He sputtered, standing on the sidewalk. "Me? *I'm* dramatic?"

"Yes," Sara and I said together.

I tugged on his sleeve. "Is this the diner?" In front of us was a brick building painted a light olive green. Red letters in the window proclaimed it to have the best cup of coffee in Tennessee. I hoped the hot chocolate was good too. Before I had left home, I had shoved all my birthday money in my pockets. I was going to buy the biggest stack of pancakes and ask for all the whipped cream.

Raymond took a deep breath. He smoothed his hair and then wiped his palms on his pants legs.

"You okay?" I asked.

"Did you tell her?" Sara asked, pausing just beside Raymond.

"Tell me what?"

Raymond sighed. "Listen, okay," he said, "they really like me here."

"*Oh*-kay." I stretched out the word. He nodded at me, eyes wide, and then opened the door.

Chapter Eighteen

A light-up sign in a diner window proclaimed it was HOME OF TENNESSEE'S BEST BBQ CONTEST.

A bell rang as Raymond opened the door.

Inside, it was bright, with music from the fifties blasting from a real jukebox in the corner. The long room was full of Formica tables with metal trim and stuffed vinyl benches, all in shades of green. The floor was a light-colored linoleum. The wait staff wore olive-green dresses or pants with aprons stuffed with napkins, straws, pens, and order pads. If they weren't taking orders, they were singing while carrying trays overflowing with breakfast and lunch. The kitchen was open to the restaurant, and three cooks worked over steaming griddles. It was a typical diner, I thought, wondering at Raymond's peculiar love for the place, and why he said everyone liked him.

And then I saw it.

"Raymond," I whispered, "why is your picture framed and hanging on the wall?"

Beside me, Sara laughed. "Just wait."

In the middle of the room was a huge photograph of Raymond, smiling into the camera, a half-dozen waitresses around him with their heads held close to his. Beside it were four other framed pictures, all of Raymond through the past few years, all with him surrounded by waitresses.

Raymond shrugged. "I told you, they like me here."

Almost as if they were tuned in to his voice, a few waitresses turned toward us. They gasped. "Y'all! It's Raymond Day!" one of the cooks called out, and the staff members cheered.

"*Ray*mond Day! *Ray*mond Day! *Ray*mond Day!"

The waitresses rushed forward, hugging Raymond and pinching his cheeks. Then, wrapping their arms around him, they ushered him to a booth. "All right!" one of the waitresses called, pulling a chair from the bar and standing on it. "Raymond's here, so it's time for our annual barbecue eating contest!"

Barbecue eating contest? It was barely nine in the morning!

Sara slid into a booth, and I sat across from her. After his cheeks were pinched for a while, Raymond joined us, sitting next to me.

Patrons and wait staff cheered. All but one person, a huge older man. He growled and slammed his fists on the tabletop, making his platter of scrambled eggs quiver. The man threw some money on the table, still grumbling, and stomped out of the room. An older waitress waved with her fingertips at his retreating back, and then turned to Raymond.

I rubbed at my tired eyes as a different waitress tied a plastic bib around Raymond's neck. "Ready, sweetheart?" she asked him.

"You bet!" Raymond held his fork in one hand and his knife in the other.

The entire restaurant cheered. Sara sighed. "Again," she muttered, "I'm internally eye rolling."

"Anyone want to take on Raymond as Little Bass Barbecue Champion?" the waitress bellowed.

Silence all around. No one moved, not one person. Raymond's head swiveled to take it all in.

I started to raise my hand. Raymond kicked me under the table. I lowered it.

"Wonderful!" The waitress clapped her hands, along with everyone else. "Once again, Raymond is our uncontested champion!"

Coming out from the kitchen, a cook brought a heaping platter of ribs coated with dry rub, a pile of smoked pork with tomato-red sauce, and a dollop of coleslaw. "Here you go, Raymond! Welcome back!"

Raymond grinned and dug his fork into the barbecue as everyone cheered his name. "*Ray*mond! *Ray*mond! *Ray*-mond!" This continued until he ate a bite from every portion. Then the waitresses squeezed his shoulder, and one by one went to their other tables.

"Want some?" Raymond asked.

I slapped the table with my palms. "Raymond Crickett, what is going on?"

Raymond pushed the plate toward me, and I nabbed the biscuit. Raymond shrugged and scooped up another bite of barbecue. "It started a couple of years ago." He wiped at his mouth. "I'm going to go see if Cheryl has any hot chocolate. The barbecue's great, but I was in the mood for pancakes. Want anything?"

"Uh, sure. Pancakes and bacon sound great."

"Eggs Benedict. Spinach. Hollandaise on the side," Sara piped in.

"Cool," Raymond said. A few people walked by, and they gave him hugs and fist bumps. "I'll be right back."

I rubbed my eyes just to make sure I was seeing what I was seeing. And I was. Raymond Crickett was a hero here. "What's going on?" I asked Sara. "Why is Raymond so popular?"

The waitress passing by was about Gran's age. She winked at me. "Isn't he just the cutest?" I didn't know how to answer that, so I didn't.

Sara laughed. "I can't believe he didn't tell you."

"I'm beginning to think I don't know him very well at all."

"Helen," Sara called over her shoulder to the waitress. "Can you fill in Trixy on why you love Raymond so much?" Sara pulled out her phone and reinserted her earbuds.

The waitress smiled. Her teeth were so bright white and straight, they couldn't be real. As she slid into the bench across from me, she patted my hand. "Well," she said in a soft drawl, "let's start at the beginning. About five years ago, this little boy walks into the diner on about the worst day we had. But I'm going to have to back up a bit. You see, Fred"—she thumbed behind her toward the kitchen—"and I opened this here diner about forty years ago. At that time, the town was booming. We had more customers than you could shake a stick at. Oftentimes, we had to do just that." She chuckled. "We also had a dozen bars up and down the street and sometimes things got rowdy." The woman leaned back and blew out her breath like those memories were gnats to scatter.

"Little did we know," she said, "those were Little Bass's glory days, such as they were. Businesses began to close, folks moved toward Memphis. Population dwindled."

"Was that when the orphanage closed?" I asked.

"Orphanage?" Her forehead wrinkled. "Oh, the Society for Friendless Children! You're mixed up on time, darling. That orphanage closed for good in the 1960s. I went to school with a couple of the girls."

I thought again about Raymond saying Gran was *old.* "Do you remember Dollie? Dollie Jacobs?"

She shook her head. "Sweetheart, I was ten years old then. Little Bass folks didn't mix much with the orphanage kids."

"Oh," I said. For a moment neither of us spoke, and then another cheer went up for Raymond by the bar. "So, what happened next?" I prompted. "You said the population was dwindling?"

"Right," Helen said. "Soon we were the only restaurant in town, but even so Fred and I kept up with traditions we started in the busy days, including our annual barbecue eating contest. Fred makes the best dry rub in the state, bar none. Each year, we'd hold a contest. Whoever could eat the most platters would win free barbecue for the whole year."

Helen sighed. "Well, like I said, hard times befell most businesses that year. Lots of folks too. But not Georgie

Gardner. That old stick in the mud was fine as a pig in spring, raking in money from the investments his son arranged for him. Old Georgie has a hollow gut; he could eat more platters of barbecue than anyone could imagine. Four, five, six platters. *Poof*, gone!" Helen's jaw set. Her arms wobbled as she waved them, miming placing more and more platters in front of me.

Her finger jabbed the air between us. "Know what's worse? That Old Georgie came back *every* meal for barbecue. We tried to tell him *free barbecue for a year* meant once a week, not three meals a day. But he said 'ain't no rules printed,' so we were responsible. The only verbiage was the sign, and it said *free barbecue for a year*." Helen's teeth ground together as though chewing back what she really wanted to say about Old Georgie. "And each time he came in, he ate like the contest was ongoing. More and more and more. So here we were, the only restaurant in town, and we were about to be run out of business, thanks to the one person who could afford to pay his bills."

"I bet my gran could've beaten him," I said, thinking about the spinach. "Why didn't you just cancel the contest?"

"Well, *hope*, I guess." Helen took a deep breath and smoothed her hands on the table. "Fred there wanted the diner to be on the map. You know, the one that the state puts out at rest stops every year? Only way he could is if we had something special. The contest was it. Only person I know more stubborn than Old Georgie is Fred.

"So, it was the one-year anniversary of the barbecue contest, right?" Helen said, a smile flickering across her face. "That stick-in-the-mud shows up for breakfast, like usual, and polishes off two platters of barbecue, even though the contest wouldn't be till lunchtime. That's how confident he was in his hollow gut. At noon, of course, he was back.

"We announce the contest is beginning"—Helen gestured toward the bar chair she had just used to do the same proclamation—"and of course no one even bothers to go up against Old Georgie. I told you, it was a bad time. So bad, in fact, that along with announcing that the winner would get free barbecue for a year, I added, 'Or as long as we're open.' We couldn't get ends to meet. We were in real trouble. Everyone felt it. All except this pip-squeak kid. Raymond couldn't have been more than six years old. He came in here entirely on his own."

Sara glanced up then. "I actually was here," she muttered. "The cane sometimes renders me invisible, I guess."

Helen held up a finger, went behind the bar and grabbed a pot of coffee, topped off about a half dozen cups on the way back to our table, and then flipped the upside-down mug in front of herself and filled it with the dark brew. She sipped it.

"Raymond was here?" I prompted.

Helen nodded. "Yep. When he heard us announcing the contest—free barbecue for a year—he raised his hand to participate." She laughed. "I told him, 'You don't win, and you'll have to pay for your food, son.' And you know what he said back?"

I shook my head, and she laughed again. "He said, 'But I don't pay if I win, right?' When I said yes, he replied, 'Then I'm gonna win.'"

I looked over to Raymond, who still stood by the bar. He was getting selfies with the different waitresses. I closed my eyes, remembering back to when we were six. "That was the year after their mama left," I whispered.

Sara nudged Helen. "I've got to go wash my hands."

Helen settled back down after Sara left. "He told me that—about his mama leaving—a couple of years later. Raymond said his dad was forgetful that year. I think more like he didn't know better yet. He didn't think, for example, to give his kids a little cash before sending them into the diner." Helen smiled. "Now they're peas in a pod, don't get me wrong. But poor Raymond thought he was on his own."

"So, what did he do?" I asked.

Raymond, now standing behind me, answered. "I ate four platters of barbecue."

Helen hooted and clapped. "Which was one more than Old Georgie."

"How did you do it?" I asked.

"Well, you just had to finish a platter." Raymond, his cheeks pink and glowing, sat beside me. "So, when I couldn't finish it myself, I went around the diner, giving people whatever they wanted." He shrugged.

Helen slurped her coffee. "Old Georgie was mad about that, let me tell you! But I just told him what he had said to me: 'Ain't no rules printed.'"

"Didn't Georgie try it too?"

"Yes, he did." Helen snorted. "Once he finally looked up from his platter and saw what was happening. But not one person in Little Bass would take so much as a biscuit off his plate." She leaned forward and ruffled Raymond's hair. "But that's not all he did to save the diner." Helen pushed out of the booth as Sara returned. She came back a moment later holding a framed picture. It was Raymond, his front teeth missing and his smile huge, on stage at a concert. His dad was behind him, holding a fiddle to his shoulder.

Helen pointed to the chubby-faced Raymond. "This boy broke out on stage during his daddy's concert—right in the middle of 'Devil Went Down to Georgia'—and told everyone the best barbecue in Texas was in Little Bass."

"But we're in Tennessee," I pointed out as both Helen and Raymond laughed.

"I think that's what piqued so many folks' interest!" She squeezed Raymond's shoulder. "The diner was packed for weeks. This boy didn't know what he was doing from the get-go. But he saved us."

Chapter Nineteen

Only one of Gran's stories ever scared me. It was one she told me when I had been crying that I wished Mama and Daddy would have another baby, so I could be a big sister too.

Gran had laughed. "Why in the world would you want that?"

"Because you always had each other," I said. "I'm forever alone."

Gran elbowed me in the side. "Oh, I'm invisible now?"

"You know what I mean," I had said.

Gran told me this story then, and I never asked for a baby brother or sister again. In fact, that night, I had crawled into her bed, curling around her with my head buried in her hair.

At the Society for Friendless Children, residents were allowed visitors every Sunday afternoon.

Dollie and Lil Sis never had a visitor. Aunt Elise had written letters a few times, but Dollie had thrown them out, unread, telling Lil Sis they didn't need anyone but each other. So, Sunday afternoons, they would go out onto the playground swings and twist the chains into tight circles, letting them spin them around again and again, while the other girls got trinkets and hugs in the cafeteria, and promises that they wouldn't be in the Home forever. That someday they'd go home.

But this Sunday one of the Clackers called them to the cafeteria. "You have visitors," she said.

Lil Sis popped up and ran from the swings before Dollie could get hers untwisted. "I bet it's Henry!" Lil Sis yelled over her shoulder.

Dollie fell as she scrambled free from the swing chains. She rushed toward Lil Sis, trying to stop her, to save her from being disappointed. Lil Sis sprinted to the cafeteria, skidding to a halt when she spotted who was waiting for them behind Miss Winters.

Mother.

And Aunt Elise.

Miss Winters clasped her hands in front of her. Her smile was tight. "Hello, girls."

Aunt Elise's arms floated toward them for a moment, as though they'd run toward her. As though she'd hug them if they did. Dollie squeezed Lil Sis's shoulders, but Lil Sis didn't move toward either of them.

It was harder for Dollie to look at Mother, who stood a few feet to the left and behind Aunt Elise. She wore little blue gloves, and a dress with a matching jacket. Her hair was styled into a bun, and her lips painted bright red. "Surprise," she said, her voice huskier than last time they had heard it. She fished a cigarette out from her small purse.

Mother sighed. "My husband says I can only take one. I'll take the little one." She held out a gloved hand for Lil Sis. Though Lil Sis didn't move, Dollie's hands curled into her shoulders.

"Your husband?" Dollie repeated.

"Father's here?" Lil Sis went up on tiptoes, peering out the cafeteria windows.

Mother snorted, puffing out smoke. "No." She

smoothed her hair with her hand. "I haven't seen your father in a long time. I'm remarried." She inhaled again. "You have a new father now."

Lil Sis leaned against Dollie.

Aunt Elise cleared her throat. She turned so she wasn't facing Mother. "I'm prepared to take them both." She clapped her hands against her legs. "I worked it all out. With the extra income, we should be just fine. The neighborhood issue we had before won't be a problem. The boy, Henry, told his parents they overreacted. It was all a misunderstanding. I'll take both girls." Again, her arms floated toward them. This time, Dollie *did* hold Lil Sis in place.

Mother stubbed out the cigarette onto the table. "You just want the money, Elise. Admit it!"

"How dare—" Aunt Elise whipped toward Mother.

"Well, you can't have it! They're mine," Mother snapped. "Mine!"

"Fine job you've done of showing that!" Aunt Elise snapped back. Dollie shifted so Lil Sis was behind her.

"I'm here now." Mother crossed her arms and focused on Miss Winters. "I want the little one." She held out a hand to Lil Sis. "Let's go."

Lil Sis whimpered. Dollie shook her head. "What money?" she asked.

"Miss Winters here, little detective that she is, found your father," Mother said. "During the past two years, he got himself a new family. A new job. And a judge just ordered that he has to send money to take care of *all* his children." She smiled. "His aunt is under the impression *she's* getting that money."

Miss Winters held up her hands. "This isn't about money."

Mother snorted again. "Of course it's about money."

"It's about what's best for the girls," Miss Winters said as though Mother hadn't spoken. "It'd be best for them to stay together."

Mother smiled. "You don't get to make any decisions, and neither do they. They're *my* daughters. I'm taking one of them."

Next to her, Aunt Elise's face flushed red. She wiped at her cheeks. "Have you no soul?"

Mother pointed to Lil Sis. "Go, gather your things. We're leaving."

Lil Sis trembled so hard that Dollie had no choice but to stand firm. "No."

Dollie lifted her chin, her face as set as when she faced down Madame Brick. For the briefest moment, Mother and Aunt Elise shared a glance, their eyes wide. Miss Winters's mouth twitched. "No," Dollie said again. "Lil Sis is going to go with Aunt Elise. *I'll* go with you."

"No, Dollie!" Lil Sis squeaked.

"What makes you think you're in charge?" Mother asked.

Dollie didn't look down at her little sister. Her chin lifted even higher. "I kept her safe. I looked after her. And if you're going to take her away from me, I'm telling you where she goes, and it isn't with you."

Lil Sis whimpered. "No, Dollie. I want to go with you."

Dollie snorted, sounding too much like Mother. "What we want doesn't matter, not until we're grown-ups." She pushed Lil Sis away from her. "You'll be happy with Aunt Elise."

Lil Sis rushed back, clinging to her, burying her face in Dollie's side. "I need you! I need *you*!" Dollie stepped away as Miss Winters pulled Lil Sis from her arms.

Moments later, Dollie left the Society for

Friendless Children. She didn't say good-bye to Lil Sis, now crying but wrapped in Aunt Elise's arms. She didn't look back at the Home, where Sallie stared at her through an upstairs window.

She followed Mother down the steps and into her new life.

Chapter Twenty

When we finished our breakfast, Raymond got his picture taken again with the waitresses. I tried to pay for my pancakes, but Helen refused to take the money. "Any friend of Raymond is on the house," she said. I offered to take a photograph with her too, but she just laughed and gave Raymond another hug.

While they were doing all of that, I told Sara that I wanted to check out the orphanage where Gran used to live.

"Oh, yeah," Sara said. "I just remembered. She told me about that place."

"What?" I nearly choked on one last bite of pancake.

Sara shrugged. "She told me she had lived in an orphanage in Little Bass. Said that was why she recommended the town to Dad. Thought maybe she'd come along and check it out someday. Bring you too."

I chewed on that for a bit. *Gran told Sara about it too.*

Sara looked up the address of the old Society for Friendless Children on her phone. "What a name," she murmured. "Think they have room for me?"

I snickered. "That's what Raymond said about us."

Sara snorted. I had a feeling that was her replacement move for rolling her eyes. "Yeah, sure. You just saw Raymond. He gets whatever he wants."

That made me sit back a little. *Raymond?* Getting whatever he wanted? Unless it was to be ignored or picked on at school, I didn't think that was the case.

Sara turned on audio directions on her phone as we left the diner, listening as it told us where to turn.

"Raymond," I said, and again we trailed behind Sara, "why didn't you tell me about the diner?"

According to Sara's Google search, the Society was now a senior center. We had told Mr. Crickett we'd be back by noon, and it was after ten. Hopefully it wouldn't take too long to get to the center.

"I *did* tell you about the diner," he replied.

I nudged his side with my elbow. "You told me you liked the diner, but you didn't tell me you were a hero! You didn't tell me the story about it."

Sara directed us across the street. The town of Little Bass seemed to flow out from a traffic circle with big pine trees and a statue of someone on horseback. We waited for the walk symbol before crossing even though there weren't any cars coming. The Cricketts are rule followers like that.

Raymond said, "If I had told you that I had saved a restaurant, and that everyone cheered when I walked in, would you have believed me?"

"Of course I would've," I said. But the words fell like pebbles in front of us, quickly kicked away.

"You wouldn't," Raymond said. "And anyone who heard me telling you would've made fun of me." He shrugged. "Sometimes you've got to keep something locked up until the right person doesn't just *hear* it; they're part of it."

"We're still talking about the diner, right?" I asked.

"Right."

We didn't talk as we waited again for the walk symbol to move forward. "How does she know?" I asked Raymond, nodding toward his sister.

"I hear it," Sara snapped. Sure enough, the walk symbol also emitted a little beeping sound.

"But you said on the bus that you don't have super hearing," I blurted. "'Cause I thought that was the case. Like because your eyes are bad, you get super hearing?"

"The only thing I get is super annoyed." Sara's cane

clacked against the crosswalk a little louder than before. "And my eyes aren't *bad*. Nothing about a body can be good or bad. My eyes just work differently than yours."

Once we were across, Raymond whispered, "She doesn't hear any better than you. She just uses her hearing in ways you don't."

The tall brick building no longer had a sign declaring it the Society for Friendless Children out front. Now it read LITTLE BASS SENIOR CENTER. The stairway where a dozen girls in matching plain dresses, closely cropped hair, and steady expressions had lined up for a group photograph now sported a wheelchair ramp curling up the side. Cheerful country swing music trickled out from its open double doors.

"All right," Sara said, and pointed to a large oak tree. "I'm going to go over there in the shade while y'all Scooby-Doo whatever it is that you're doing."

Raymond was on the third step before he realized I wasn't behind him. My feet had turned to anchors, digging deep into the dry ground at the base of the stairs. I squinted toward the farthest corner of the steps, picturing the fierce girl with her arm around her little sister. How had she marched out of those doors with her head high, alone? Did I want to find out the rest of that story? *Would* I find out more of the story? The Society had closed for good nearly sixty years ago. Dollie and Lil Sis left it in the early 1950s.

A woman using a walker laughed so hard she leaned into a tall, thin woman with white hair as they moved into the building. The music combined with their laughter. The lights were on and the whole center looked cozy and bright. If the people flowing in and out of the rooms inside were younger, this is how I first had pictured the Home when Gran shared stories about it. Maybe because that's how *my* life had been, and I wanted that for her.

But once I made the stories mine too, I realized how different it must've been for her. Dull and cold. Scary.

Raymond still stood on that third step. "Are you coming, Trixy?"

I followed him to the top.

The doors opened to a wide hallway. On one side was a wide room with a polished wood floor and high ceilings. *The gymnasium*, I realized, *where Dollie, Lil Sis, and the other girls watched movies*. Now it had circular tables with people painting on easels. At the front was a woman in an apron, showing the artists what to add to the canvases.

On the other side of the hall was a narrower room with hanging light fixtures. *The dining room*. I pictured a long wooden table with girls scraping mounds of spinach from one plate to another. Now it had collapsible plastic tables with puzzle pieces spread across it. A couple of older men combed through the pieces. Windows along the far side overlooked a courtyard, which had once been a playground.

Raymond nudged me and pointed to framed pictures hanging farther down the hall. They were a series of class pictures from the Society for Friendless Children. I rushed down the line, looking for the one I had seen in the box of Gran's things. There it was! Dollie, her arm around Lil Sis's shoulder, peered back at me.

I kept my eyes on the little girls. Somehow seeing the photograph here, in the actual building, was making something unfurl inside me. My stomach bubbled but not in the boiling way it had been before I started writing Gran's stories. This felt more like a rustling.

We moved farther down the hall. To the right were a large bathroom and smaller rooms with closets. To the left was a huge room. It had bookshelves lining the walls. I squinted. A dormitory, with a long row of twin-sized beds, dark stockings hung to dry from the footboards.

Clack, clack, clack.

I thought at first my ears had grown so powerful they heard the past, but when Raymond turned, I knew they were actual footsteps. There in front of me wasn't one of Dollie's Clackers. Instead it was a Black woman in her eighties, her hair silvery gray. She wore a bright purple sweater and black slacks.

"May I help you?" she asked. I noticed a name tag pinned to her sweater. *Sallie.* I gasped, my eyes darting across her face, trying to connect it with the solemn girl I had seen standing beside Dollie and Lil Sis in the photo.

Was it possible?

Miss Sallie led us across the hall and gestured for us to sit at a round table in the middle of one of the smaller rooms. The windows overlooked the front steps. A coffeepot sputtered on a counter along the side of the room. I felt a pang deep in my stomach and thought of Mama, sitting at the scrubbed-clean kitchen table, a cup of coffee in her hand. I swallowed the ache as Miss Sallie took the seat across from us.

"Are you Sallie from when my gran and her sister—Dollie and Lil Sis—lived here?" I asked, not wasting time explaining who I was or why I was there.

Now that she was seated across from me, I saw the fine lines edging Miss Sallie's eyes and deeper vertical ones on either side of her mouth. "That, I am. I'm in pretty good shape for the condition I'm in, I'd say." She laughed and patted my hand with her own, the knuckles swollen. "I'd've figured out who you were the moment you smiled, before you ever mentioned Dollie and Lil Sis. You look just like them. You're a Jacobs girl, for sure."

"Yes, ma'am." I thought of the picture hanging in the hall, of Dollie with her stern face and blazing eyes. I looked nothing like her. "That's kind of you," I said, but my mind snagged on how she said "them." That rustling in my chest settled and stilled. Mama was wrong; Lil Sis was *real.*

"But that would make you more than eighty years old!" Mr. Obvious Raymond Crickett observed.

"Nevertheless, I'm finer than a frog hair split three ways," she said, her chin up high.

Raymond gasped and elbowed me. "Hey! Trixy says that sometimes."

I elbowed him back. "That's because Gran used to say it."

Miss Sallie nodded, then curled her hands around the steaming coffee mug. "I imagine she's why you're here," she said. "This happens sometimes. Folks stop by asking about relatives who were residents of the Society. Usually, best I can do is direct them to the photographs. The Society was strict about having annual pictures. I'm in seven of them, right up until I turned eighteen and stopped being a resident and started being a—"

"You were a Clacker?" I blurted. Raymond gasped again.

Miss Sallie laughed so hard her shoulders shook. "She

told you stories 'bout the Home then, didn't she?"

I nodded as she wiped the corners of her eyes. "Nah, I wasn't a Clacker. The Society stopped taking new residents when I was about thirteen. There was a big push to move us into foster care after some shady stories about other Homes surfaced." She shuddered. "It dwindled down to just a few of us by the time I was about to age out. Then Miss Winters took me on as a housekeeper, and the Society transitioned into an office building. I sure was happy when it went to being a senior center. Seems like this old place became a home for me after all."

I heard the moment she used a lowercase *h*.

"When relatives come by asking about former residents, I help the best I can. But my memory is not what it once was, and girls came through here like water through a sieve. Only a few I remember. The Jacobs girls, I could never forget."

"Gran remembered you too," I said. "She told me you were her friend."

Miss Sallie patted my hand again. Then she looked me straight in the face. "The fact that you're here and she's not, that means she's not with this world anymore." I didn't say anything. Raymond shuffled closer to me in his seat.

"Answer me this," Miss Sallie said, her voice low. "Was she happy?"

I closed my eyes, remembering Gran. Picturing her dancing on the porch to Mr. Crickett's music. Filling Mama's plate. Whispering a story into my ear. Laughing at Daddy's jokes. Smiling up at the stars at night. Tears scalded my cheeks as I met Miss Sallie's eyes. "She made sure everyone around her was happy."

Miss Sallie let out a long breath. "Sounds about right."

Miss Sallie got up and added sugar to her coffee. When she came back, her eyes were red. "Saddest thing I ever saw was Dollie and Lil Sis saying good-bye to each other, Dollie heading north to Pennsylvania with her mother and Lil Sis going east to Nashville."

"Dollie went to Pennsylvania?" I swallowed. That was so far from Lil Sis. "Wait," I said, shaking my head. "They didn't say good-bye. Gran told me this story. She said she walked out of the Home with her chin up and didn't look back."

Miss Sallie grunted. "That's something Dollie would say. Weren't the case, though." She flattened her hands on the table as though steadying herself. "When Lil Sis realized one of them would be going one way and the other another, a wail like I never heard rumbled through this Home, accustomed though it was to girls' tears. Can you imagine what that sounded like?"

Raymond shook his head, but I nodded. I did know a

wail like that. One had ripped from me the morning after the accident. And I had heard the echoes of another, just a few months before that. Gran's hush-hush story trembled deep inside me. I swallowed it down.

Miss Sallie took a big breath. My ears tingled with an incoming story, but Miss Sallie spoke it at the same time. I wasn't surprised to hear it in tandem—her shaking old lady voice and the whisper of the little girl she once had been. "The other girls who didn't have visitors that day and I were out on the playground. Hearing that wail, I ran back into the building. Miss Winters had told their mother and aunt that they'd have to wait while the girls packed and the adults filled out paperwork. Instead, she brought Dollie and Lil Sis here, into this room."

I shivered and Raymond gasped a third time. I elbowed his side. "*Dramatic,*" I whispered, and he shut his mouth.

Miss Sallie didn't seem to have noticed; she was nearly seventy years away. "I should've given them their privacy. I know that." She nodded to herself, eyes drifting to a corner behind me, and I knew that's where Dollie and Lil Sis must've clung to each other. "But I never had a sister." She took a deep breath, and then turned her head toward the window. "Dollie had never cried, not once, during the nearly two years they spent here at the Society. Even when Madame Brick made her spend hours alone in the basement, all lights off, while we laughed along to *Pinocchio*, she came out of that cold, dark space with dry cheeks and upturned chin."

"Wait, she was punished?" I cut in. "For the spinach?"

"She *did* tell you stories, didn't she?" Miss Sallie laughed.

I nodded and said, "But she didn't tell me about the basement. She told it to me like it was a funny story."

"That's how she was with Lil Sis, always making things brighter for her." A sad smile twitched on Miss Sallie's face. "Madame Brick could be creative with her punishments. I cleaned down in that basement years later, when I was a grown woman. Someone didn't know I was down there and flipped the lights out." She shuddered. "Oh, I screamed! I barreled up those stairs so quick I nearly left the Holy Spirit behind! How that little girl managed to sit down there alone for two hours, I don't know, but she came out looking bold as day."

"I told you it was sad," Raymond whispered.

Miss Sallie nodded. "A lot of times it was, for sure. But our lives weren't happy outside the Home, were they? At least when we were in these walls, we had each other. Dollie understood that here, at least we knew the rules, had some control. She made sure Lil Sis learned."

"What happened," I asked, "when they said good-bye?"

Miss Sallie sipped her coffee and swallowed hard.

"Dollie broke." Her voice hitched. "She cried, and for the first time ever, I saw Lil Sis support *her*. She took her hand and pulled her over to the window. By then, it was early evening. The first stars were beginning to shine. Lil Sis pointed to the brightest one. 'Every night,' she said, 'every single night, you look up at that star and you tell me you love me, and I'll tell the same star I love you.'" Miss Sallie didn't bother wiping at the tear that slid down her cheek, so I didn't catch mine either.

Miss Sallie continued. "Dollie told her it didn't matter. Her ears would never hear the words. Lil Sis put a hand on each side of Dollie's face. 'There's magic in stars,' she said. 'You don't know this, because you didn't see the movie. But I did, and there's magic in stars. It'll make your ears hear me, and I'll hear you.'"

This time, I was the one who gasped.

"What are you doing?" I had asked Gran as she stared up at the brightest star in the sky.

"Oh, nothing," Gran had said, a smile tugging at her cheeks. "Just telling her I love her."

"The star?"

She hadn't corrected me, but she hadn't been whispering to a star. She had been talking to her sister.

Chapter Twenty-One

As we walked back through Little Bass toward the hotel, I pondered what Miss Sallie had shared with me. I pictured Dollie crouching alone in a dark basement while everyone else watched the movie. I remembered all of the times Gran had sung that silly song about wishing on a star. I thought about how she always whispered to the brightest star at night.

Raymond didn't say anything until we were through the little traffic circle and back in front of the hotel.

"You two okay?" Sara asked us. I didn't know a whole lot about Raymond's sister, but I was starting to understand that she wasn't one to pry.

I shrugged.

"It's Trixy," Raymond said. "She just found out Gran's stories aren't true."

I moved to slap at his arm before remembering that it was just how Mama would react when Daddy said something ridiculous. "What are you talking about, Raymond Crickett? Miss Sallie *confirmed* that Lil Sis and Dollie were real, and that they did all of the things in the stories."

Raymond stilled, looking for all the world like I *had* slapped him. "No, Trixy," he said. "They're real, but the stories aren't *true.*"

"Of course they're true! Why would you say something like that?"

Raymond actually looked confused. "Because Gran didn't tell you right. She didn't tell you about having to go to the basement over the spinach. She didn't tell you about saying good-bye to Lil Sis. She didn't tell you the *truth*."

I lifted my chin. "She told me *a* truth."

"There's no such thing," Raymond insisted. "Truth is truth."

Sara unsnapped her cane, folded it up, and tucked in into her bag. "Not to go for the obvious metaphor here, but maybe Gran just saw things differently."

The hotel lobby was full of skinny men with fancy beards. "Dad's band," Raymond muttered as I looked around.

"They all have just enough beards and tattoos to look like they're melding into each other," Sara said. She laughed. "Faces kind of look like blurs to me from a distance. I can pick out Dad in a crowd—usually—by looking for his shape plus the dark smudges of tattoos on his arms and beard on his face. But the Crickett Quintet is a bunch of similarly shaped men with smudgy arms and faces."

"Oh," I said, remembering being three and hugging Mom's legs at a carnival, only to look up and see it was a different woman wearing a similar red skirt. "That must be frustrating."

Sara shrugged. "Yeah. Too bad he couldn't be into punk. A mohawk would've been a lot more distinctive."

"How do you find me?" I asked.

"Find you? I can't seem to shake you, kid," Sara said, but she gently punched my shoulder. "And aside from being small and loud, you wear a lot of purple," she added, her voice softer. "Gran always wore purple too."

"It's our favorite color," I whispered. "I'm sorry about what I said earlier. About your eyes being bad. I know that's not—"

"I know," Sara said. "And thank you."

Mohawk-less Mr. Crickett was sprawled on a rocking chair farthest from the front door. He was checking the strings of his fiddle while the other players talked like it had been blasting day at the quarry. Maybe all the loud music had the same effect on their hearing.

"All right," Mr. Crickett said as Raymond and I approached. "Did you load up on fame at the diner?" he asked Raymond.

Raymond smiled and nodded. Mr. Crickett winked at him and then seemed to remember how mad he was at us both. The smile faded from his face.

"Did you pick up another kid?" one of the band members guffawed.

Mr. Crickett jerked his chin in my direction. "This here is Trixy Mae Williams. She's road-tripping with us for the next few days." To the rest of the band, he said, "Let's get a move on, head on into Memphis."

As we walked toward the truck, Mr. Crickett grinned. "How about you sit up on the seat this time, Trixy?" He seemed like the kind of person who had a tough time staying angry at anyone. Maybe that's why Raymond was such a forgiving friend.

That evening, while the band warmed up, Sara, Raymond, and I had an early dinner at the restaurant where his dad would be playing that night. It was another barbecue joint. All the seating was outside, curling around a wide-open area used as a stage. Strings of yellow café lights crisscrossed overhead. People went through carrying their barbecue on plastic trays and drinking pop from waxed paper cups. We sat in the back at a table built around a fireplace. Before too long I could look at the stars.

I'm listening, Gran, I whispered to the brightest one. The band launched into an upbeat song and Raymond grabbed my hand. "Let's dance!" he said, and tried to tug me up to my feet.

"No way." I laughed. "I don't dance." The music playing was so fast—how could anyone keep the beat?

"That's the greatest thing about being far from home," Raymond said. "We'll never see any of these people again. Besides, I noticed something going to all these concerts. No one dances until the first two people start. Then it's contagious."

"I can't dance to country swing," I told him.

"Sure, you can! Box step, just like gym class." Raymond had been my partner during the square dance section of gym. Everyone groaned whenever we had to practice at school, but when I told Gran about it, she had been delighted. For weeks, she clapped the rhythm and sang while Raymond and I danced on the porch over and over. Sara, having benefited from four more years of gym-class square dance instruction, coached us along.

Then Mr. Crickett taught us flat-footing, a way to jig

along to bluegrass music. That whole summer, we made the porch rattle with our dancing.

Funny to think how much could change in a few years. But maybe I remembered the steps. Raymond tugged my hand again, and we twirled across the open dance floor. Some people laughed and others clapped. Raymond tilted his head a moment later as an old couple held each other and danced next to us. "Told you others would join in."

One of his hands held my hand up and to the side; the other rested on my waist. Henry and Lil Sis did this too, the day of the bees. I wondered if she laughed when he twirled her, the way I did now. I spun around and grabbed Sara's hand. She was sitting at the table, looking at her phone. I noticed other patrons had been nudging one another when she did that, as though someone who used a cane wouldn't be able to also use her phone. Sara hadn't seemed to notice, except that she stopped looking around. I had never considered what it must be like for Sara to not see *everything* everyone else saw, but to see enough that other people felt entitled to question the gaps.

"Dance with us!" I told her.

Sara sighed. "I don't dance."

"Sure you do!" I pulled her upright and linked my arm in hers. "Remember? You taught us!"

Raymond laughed and grabbed her other arm. The two

of us kick-stepped to the beat as Sara shook her head. After a few seconds, she couldn't resist and started moving along with us, even laughing a little. Raymond spun her and soon the two of them faced each other, clogging the way they had years earlier when they were on the porch, but instead of Gran, I was the one clapping to the beat.

The song ended and Mr. Crickett put down his fiddle and moved to the microphone. The band slowed the tempo. Another band member clapped his hands against the stool in front of him to keep beat. Soon Mr. Crickett was singing about this being oh, what a wonderful world as he looked out over the dance floor at his children. Sara and Raymond kept spinning each other around and around.

I sat at the table again, missing Gran down to my bones. I missed Daddy and hoped he was okay. And I ached for Mama too, missing who she was before she had started to fade away.

After the concert, we went back to the hotel. My eardrums felt like they were still being plucked by strings. A huge bridge shaped like a melting letter *m* was lit to look bright blue. Everywhere cars wove in and out of the highways. Around us, the city lights glittered like fireworks across the water. There were so many things to look at—even a pyramid right beside the highway—that I forgot to blink. Who knew such a place was just a few hours from my little house?

I wondered if Dollie had stared, wide eyed, out the window when she left with Mother, heading north for Pennsylvania. What else had she seen on that journey? Did she spend it burrowed under a blanket the way she had when she and Lil Sis had left Sweetheart Mountain? Raymond sat in the backseat next to me. He smiled. "I'm glad you're here," he said. "I always want to dance, and I've never done it before today."

"It *was* fun," Sara said, as though surprised at herself.

He mimed dancing in his seat, and I clapped my knees. Soon we were both laughing. Mr. Crickett's mouth pulled up in a smile and his ear angled toward us like a vacuum cleaner trying to suck up the laughter into himself. Raymond didn't laugh often enough.

"You were right about the dancing, but you were wrong," I told him when Mr. Crickett parked the truck in the hotel lot. He and Sara had just gotten out of the front seats. "I mean about Gran's stories not being true. Because right now? I'm happy, but I'm sad too. Both can be true."

Raymond put up his arm to stop me from getting out of the truck. "Trixy," he said, "I think you should stop now."

"What?" I said, sitting back down.

"We know that Dollie went north and Lil Sis went to Aunt Elise's. We know Gran says she lost her. We know the story ends in sadness." He took a big breath. When he opened his mouth again, his words tumbled over each other in a rush. "I don't know where my mom is. I don't know if I'll ever see her again or if I'll ever know why she left or if she ever even loved me. I don't know and I don't want to, Trixy. I don't *want to*. Because no matter what, I know it's sad. It ends sad. This story . . ." He glanced at my ears. "It ends sad."

He hopped out of the truck and started toward the hotel. I swallowed hard, then followed him.

A star was glinting in the sky. "Do you remember Gran dancing?" I asked Raymond's back. Without turning around, he nodded. "Even if Dollie and Lil Sis's story ends sad, she figured out a way to be happy again, didn't she?"

"Yeah," Raymond said. "I guess she did."

Mr. Crickett called Daddy once we were back in our room. The front desk person had wheeled in a little cot for me to sleep on next to Sara's pull-out couch since supposedly I snore. Mr. Crickett closed the door to our little room to talk to Daddy, but the doors were thin.

"Yeah, man, it's going well," Mr. Crickett said, his voice raspy from singing so much. "Honestly, it's nice having her here. Raymond's having fun. Sara too, which is a rarity. It's good to hear them palling around."

There was a long pause while Daddy talked.

"No," Mr. Crickett said. "I'm telling you, no worries. Just glad they came clean. Mostly, anyway . . . I'm not sure, but they're definitely on a mission. Sara said they spent the day at a senior center."

A few minutes later, he came back in and handed me the phone. I took a deep breath before answering. "Hey, Daddy."

"Trixy," Daddy said, and I could tell he still was sore at me. "Raymond's dad says you're behaving. That's something, at least."

Daddy told me Mama had been transferred to the treatment center that morning. "I talked with her a few minutes ago. I told her you were going with Raymond on this road trip. Left out the bit about you running away to do it."

"Oh," I said.

There was rustling on the phone as Daddy rubbed it against his chin as he thought through his words. "There's a lot of stuff I need to learn about your mama. A lot about what's going on with her that is more than it seems. Some of it's wrapped up in losing Gran. Some of it's hers. It's all mixed up."

"Doesn't seem tricky to me. It just seems like she should eat more," I said, knowing even as I said the words, they were a lie. I huffed from my nose trying to get rid of some of the anger I didn't want to feel toward Mama for scaring me and the guilt for being angry in the first place. I was glad that Daddy covered for me with Mama. Mostly. But a mean part of me also wanted her to worry about *me* instead of how many steps she had taken or how much she ate. I tried to push aside those wicked feelings.

"Trixy Mae, I raised you better than that. Don't you sass me nor talk that way about your mama. This isn't about food, not really. It's about control." More rustling. "Gran, she always did the best she could, but some things . . . like how she was so close to you but when it came to Mama, it was . . . different."

"Gran was great to everyone," I insisted.

"Yeah," Daddy said. "She was. But with you, she could just love you. With Mama, she was responsible for her, and maybe that was a different relationship."

I thought about Dollie, walking out of the Home, leaving Lil Sis behind.

I heard another story under his words, one about Gran bringing out platters and platters of food, filling up any gaps on our plates. I thought about her eating all of the spinach so no one else would get in trouble. I thought about Mama and about emptiness that can't be filled.

Chapter Twenty-Two

The next morning, Mr. Crickett whistled while he loaded the truck. Raymond, Sara, and I ate breakfast in the hotel lobby. For some reason, the happier Mr. Crickett was, the angrier Raymond and more annoyed Sara seemed to be. When Mr. Crickett rubbed Raymond's head as he walked by, Raymond salted his hard-boiled eggs so hard he dented the yolk.

"You're acting like a bee flew up your butt this morning, Raymond," I observed. Sara laughed.

"Don't say *butt*. It ain't nice." Raymond brushed some of the salt off with his fingertip.

"You just said *butt*," I pointed out, being mature enough to not correct his use of *ain't*.

"No, I repeated *butt*. You said *butt*."

"Well, we've said *butt* six times," Sara said. "I feel like I'm surrounded by butts."

Finally his lips twitched.

Butt, I mouthed.

Now he laughed, covering his mouth with his hand. Sara snorted and then chuckled alongside him. When we got back from this trip, I was going to do whatever I could to make Raymond Crickett laugh more than he ever had. Maybe even more than he ought. And not just because I owed him for sneaking me into his dad's truck.

We got into the pickup. Mr. Crickett turned the engine on and then checked his beard in the mirror, making sure the ends of the mustache curled up just right and the rest of it fell to a point. Sara snorted in that internally-rolling-her-eyes way. Mr. Crickett began whistling again as he shifted into park.

"What's wrong?" I whispered to Raymond, whose eyes narrowed.

Raymond whispered back, "Dad likes Sweetheart Mountain. A *lot*."

"What's wrong with that?" Earlier, Mr. Crickett had told us the concert that night would be a small one, at a little venue on the outskirts of Sweetheart Mountain. Only a couple of hundred people were expected to attend. "They played for hours last night; maybe he's just excited for a little break."

Raymond scowled.

I elbowed him, nudging for more information. Mr. Crickett began singing along to a country radio station. "He's excited, all right, but it isn't for a break. The place he's playing tonight—Sweetheart Sings—it's owned by a . . . woman."

I gasped, putting my hands on my cheeks. "The horror!"

"Hush up, Trixy." Raymond crossed his arms. "Her name's *Sofia*." He said the name like it would burn his mouth if he didn't say it fast. "I don't like the way he looks at her. And I don't like the way he paced around the house when he set up the details. And I 'specially don't like that he had to talk to her over and over again about it, and sometimes he shut the door while he was on the phone."

Mr. Crickett glanced at us in the rearview mirror. "Oh, almost forgot to mention," he said. "I'm meeting Sofia to, uh, go over a few details before tonight's show." He said *Sofia* like it was a chocolate on his tongue. "So y'all will be on your own for a couple of hours this afternoon."

"Okay, Mr. Crickett," I said. "That sounds good."

Raymond's nostrils flared. Sara sighed again. She put her earbuds in and turned up the music so loud I could hear it. Soon she was softly singing along.

Raymond turned his fiery eyes on me. I shrugged. "We're going to need the time to go to the bakery." He shifted his body toward the window.

I nudged him again. "Maybe she's not so bad," I whispered. "It's just a kinda date, right?"

Raymond still stared out the window, but he settled back in the seat. "He hasn't dated anyone since . . ."

"Since your mom left?" I finished. He nodded, still staring out the window. "How long ago was that?"

Raymond didn't answer for a long time. How do you count how long it's been since you've seen a parent? Years don't seem right. I haven't seen Mama in two good-night hugs, three did-you-brush-your-teeths, a dozen love-you smiles.

"Six years," he whispered. I reached out for his hand, now lying on the seat beside me, wondering at what else I'd heard in that whisper. Six Christmases, thirty-nine birthday candles, dozens of middle of the night drinks of water, a hundred scraped knees, a thousand tiny earthquakes across his chest.

"That's a long time." I squeezed his hand.

Raymond looked at his dad. "It's a long time for him

too." He sighed and flashed a sideways smile. "I guess I'm just feeling sorry for myself."

"I do that all the time," I told him. "Want me to say *butt* again?"

"Hush up, Trixy," he said, but he did laugh.

We were at Sweetheart Mountain about two hours later.

After checking in to the hotel, all four of us walked downtown. Sweetheart Mountain had a super-wide main street with parking on both sides and a big sidewalk for going to different shops. No one told the sun it was autumn in Tennessee. "It's hotter than a fevered fox in a forest fire," Mr. Crickett said as he mopped his forehead under his baseball cap.

I scanned the shops, looking for one that was a bakery or at least had once been one.

Mr. Crickett led us to a hot dog shop. We all ordered Cokes, and when the waitress came back Raymond said he'd have a hot dog with everything—diced onions, chili, and mustard. Mr. Crickett said, "That's my boy" and winked at him before ordering the same. "But hold the onions." Raymond shot me a look. I knew he was thinking *Sofia*.

A moment later, the waitress returned, her arms lined with our hot dogs in paper baskets. She tossed them in front of us and, with another four dogs to deliver, moved on to the next table. I felt cozy being there with Raymond and his family, but something heavy settled into my stomach with each bite. It felt like a fishhook being pulled deeper and deeper, trying desperately to yank me all the way back to Mama and Daddy.

A couple more days, a couple more stops—the bakery and Aunt Elise's—and then I'll be heading home. If Raymond was right, when Daddy picked me up, I'd be weighed down with even more sadness. But if *I* was right—if this was a journey Gran wanted me take so I could prove her stories were real and true—maybe when I made it home again, it'd really feel like home. I'd feel like me again. Maybe Mama would too.

After lunch, Mr. Crickett went back to the hotel to freshen up for his gig. (Raymond rolled his eyes and muttered, "He means freshen up for his date.") Sara surprised me by asking if we wanted to check out the town. "There were some pretty cool people here last year," she said. Raymond and I looked at each other but neither mentioned that we were looking for the bakery that once hosted Liberace.

A half hour later, the three of us were as damp as though we had jumped into the hotel pool, but none of

the donut shops or bakeries we found were open in 1949.
"What's with you guys?" Sara asked. "How many donuts can you two eat?"

Raymond rubbed his stomach but, being the good friend he was, said, "I probably could fit in one more. At least."

Sara shrugged. "Well, there's a pie shop. I think it's a couple of blocks from here. I went there last year while you helped Dad set up at Sweetheart Sings. There's a girl there I wouldn't mind seeing again. . . . I doubt she remembers me, though." Her cheeks flushed.

"A pie shop?" I repeated as Raymond muttered about everyone falling for someone in Sweetheart Mountain.

Sara sighed. "It was just a thought."

Raymond fanned himself with his hand. "I bet it's air conditioned."

Sara smiled. "Follow me," she said, and turned on the audio directions on her phone.

We stuck to the shady side of the street, pausing once when live music trickled out from a pub.

Sara swayed in place as we listened. I could picture her standing in the center of a stage, a huge cowboy hat on her head, singing in the middle of a spotlight.

"You should do it," I said as we continued on.

"Do what?" she asked.

"Sing. I heard you, in the truck with your dad. You're a great singer."

"I'm not much of a performer." Sara ducked her head. "I mean, I could never just stand up on stage alone."

I was going to argue but realized where we were.

We stood in front of Sweetheart Mountain Pie Shop.

The shop was a squat building, the brick painted a pastel blue with an old-fashioned roof that looked a bit like swoops of frosting on a cake. A stone driveway led to a small farmhouse in the distance. On the side of the shop were a creek and some woods. A little footpath or deer trail curved from the shop through the trees.

The front of the bakery featured huge glass windows that stretched up the first story on either side of a red door. Inside were tall, round tables and stools, and in the back was a counter covered in glass-domed pie stands.

A man wearing a chef's cap and a white apron ferried more pies from the back of the shop. A teenage girl sat on a tall stool behind the register, her focus on the phone in her hand. Both of them looked up when Raymond opened the door, rattling a little bell at the hinge. We stepped inside, and I had to fight the urge to raise my arms and bask in the cool, sugar-sweet air.

"Sara!" the girl called out, dropping her phone onto the counter and bouncing to her feet.

Sara's face split into a huge grin. Both she and Raymond needed to smile more often. "Marcia?" she asked, not quite making out the teen's face yet. "I can't believe you remember me."

The girl—Marcia—laughed and rushed forward, hugging Sara. When she backed up, she said, "Well, not many girls with white canes show up."

"Marcia!" the man in the chef's hat scolded.

"No, it's cool," Sara said with a laugh.

"Yeah, Grandad," Marcia said. "Sara knows she's visually impaired." The girls linked arms. "I've been waiting all summer for you!"

"I told you I'd be back." Sara giggled. *Sara? Giggling?* The girls started chattering as they went back to perch on stools at the counter. I rubbed at my eyes. Seemed like everyone had untold stories.

"What about you two? Can I help you?" the baker asked as we looked around from the entrance. The floor was painted pastel blue, stenciled with pink diamonds. My eyes followed the straight line of diamonds directly in front of me, all the way until they met the far wall. Raymond and I gasped at the same time at what we saw there. We darted ahead.

"The pies are over here," he said as we sprinted past.

We didn't pause. Because there, on the wall, was a

large black and white photograph of a small, magnificently dressed man. His dark hair was powdered with flour and sugar, his arms spread and head thrown back in laughter, his elaborately stitched jacket smeared with frosting and cake. Around him was a tall, old man, his hands covering his mouth; a short, plump woman, her own arms thrown to the air; and a beautiful young woman, reaching toward a cake-splattered small boy. Just behind the fancy man stood a girl with ringlets, her arms thrown up in similar joy.

Raymond pointed to the girl and gasped again, but my eyes were on the edge of the photograph, where I could just glimpse a tangle of dark curls and the profile of a girl. *Dollie.* I ran my finger along the curve of her ear.

Behind us now, the man laughed. "Not many people notice the photo before the pie."

I thought of the story and pictured a little boy twirling as cake fell all around him. "You're Baby," I said.

The smile danced on his face as he also turned toward the photograph. "No one's called me that in a long time."

Marcia scoffed. "Did you just call my granddad *Baby*?"

"Sorry," Sara said. "My brother and his friend are weirdos."

"No, that's what everyone used to call me," the baker said. Turning back to us, he added, "You can call me Gary."

I could almost hear a young woman—his mother—

gathering him in her arms after he reached up. *Let me hold you, baby!*

"That was my gran," I said to him now. I touched the photo again. "And her little sister."

Gary smiled at me, and he told me how after that day, they played music all the time, his grandmother singing along in a warbling voice. How his grandfather kept cookies under the counter for any children who wandered by.

"What a lucky girl you are," Gary said. He pointed to the picture again. "My beautiful mother. I sat by the counter—sometimes on the counter—every day of my life after that day. Now my grandbabies do."

I stood at the edge of the woods, in front of the little footpath.

Raymond slipped his hand into mine.

Together, we followed it a few hundred steps until the woods cleared. There was a tiny house, not much bigger than a shed. Half the roof had fallen in and the glass was shattered in every window. I stepped closer. Maybe somewhere there would be something—a doll or a ribbon or a moment, forever trapped in that house. Maybe I would hear *her* story, her voice. I shuddered; more and more when I thought of Gran's stories, they came to me in *my* voice, not hers.

Raymond didn't let go of my hand and he didn't move forward. "For a long time," he said, "after my mom left, I'd look for her." I sucked in my breath. Raymond rarely talked about his mom. "I don't mean on the computer or anything." His face was splotchy; he *had* looked for her there too. "I mean, in crowds. Like at the mall, or at restaurants. My dad's gigs. Most of the time, I didn't even realize I was doing it until I caught a glimpse of someone who had the same color hair or who walked the same way."

Raymond dropped my hand and crossed his arms. "You know what, though? Even if I *had* found her, it wouldn't be her. Not the *her* I knew."

I wasn't sure what Raymond was trying to tell me. But I didn't step closer to the shed. Raymond quietly left, heading back to the shop, and I stood alone on the path.

I miss you, Gran.

When I finally walked back to the shop, Sara was exchanging phone numbers with Marcia. "Same time, same place, one year from now?" Marcia asked.

Sara nodded, her face shining. "Absolutely."

We left carrying mini-pies Gary had sent with us. The air didn't feel quite as thick. A breeze even flickered by now and again.

When we got back, Mr. Crickett was waiting for us, his beard and hair slicked into place. He smelled like a pine forest. "I know you just got back, but will you be okay for a couple of hours? There's a restaurant in the lobby. You can have them charge it to our room." He cleared his throat. "I'm meeting Sofia to check on the venue."

Sara and Raymond exchanged a look. Then Raymond held up the bag of mini-pies.

"What's this?" Mr. Crickett asked, peeking inside.

Raymond shrugged. "There are five of them. If you want to come back with her for dessert." He swallowed and then smiled. "After your date."

"I . . . I'm not . . ." Mr. Crickett rubbed the back of his neck the same way Raymond had a moment earlier. When he looked up, his grin was wide. "Thanks, Ray."

Chapter Twenty-Three

That evening, after having pie with Sofia—who smiled too wide but whom I liked because she always stopped talking and turned to Raymond when he spoke—we had about a half hour before going to the next gig.

The walls of Sweetheart Sings were built like garage doors, so when open, they rolled above us. Huge metal fans along the ceiling shifted the night's heavy air back and forth. On the dance floor, women in short cutoffs and cowboy boots danced with clogging steps in sync with the bluegrass music. When the band shifted to a slow song, couples swayed around us, not really leaning into each other due to the heat.

I nudged Sara. "Uh, can I use your phone?"

She arched an eyebrow at me. "Why?"

"Sara, just give her the phone," Raymond said.

Sara stared at me a little, then handed it over. Raymond mumbled something about getting us Cokes and drifted through the crowd.

I dialed Daddy's number. He answered on the first ring. "All okay there, Trixy?"

"Yes, Daddy. I miss you."

Daddy didn't say anything for a breath. "Well, that's your own doing, isn't it?" He sighed. "And I miss you too."

I told Daddy about meeting Mr. Gary and seeing the photograph in the bakery.

"Well, your mama's doing fine. In fact, they're saying she's pretty stable, more so than she appeared to be in the hospital. She might be able to come home at the end of the week, so she can start outpatient care instead. On Saturday, I'll head to Nashville to get you by lunchtime. Then we'll drive straight home again, so I can get Mama the next day."

That would give Raymond and me the morning to find Aunt Elise's house and maybe even Henry's farm. "I can't wait to see you," I told him.

"You too, kiddo." Daddy's voice was soft. "I'm going to give you a great big hug. And then you're going to be grounded forever."

I laughed. Daddy didn't.

He cleared his throat. "We're going to put all of this behind us. Forever. No more stories, no more diets, no more nothing. We're going to start fresh and leave the past in the past."

I didn't argue with him, just said good-bye. But if starting fresh meant leaving Gran behind, then I knew I couldn't do it. The thought alone made that pebble in my chest wobble.

The next morning, Mr. Crickett wasn't in a hurry to get on the road. In fact, we had a big breakfast at a diner outside Sweetheart Mountain with Sofia. They talked so much that it took them two hours to finish their pancakes. "Shouldn't we get going?" I asked a couple of times.

"I get why you're anxious. I've only been to Nashville once," Sofia said. She was pretty, with dark skin and eyes, and a wide smile. "And I'd love to go back!"

Mr. Crickett smiled. "I'd like to go with you," he told her. "But we're going to be outside Nashville today. In—"

"Wayward," I finished for him. Last night before giving Sara her phone back, I had looked up Michaelson Canning Factory. Both it and the festival were in a little town on the outskirts of the city—Wayward, Tennessee. How perfectly Gran plotted the Cricketts' tour to go across her life without ever telling them.

Gran once told me *a story curves and folds and makes a tunnel to burrow inside someone.* I wonder how many people travel along the same curve, not knowing how their stories intersect.

"That's right," Mr. Crickett agreed. "The band's meeting at the Wayward carnival grounds at noon—and that's when your dad will be there too, Trixy. So, we'll pull in and you can hop right on into your dad's car." He turned to Sofia. "This one's not a concert. It's a festival. We won it last year, so this year, we headline it. That gig pays enough to fund the second half of our tour."

"I wish I could be there to see you play." Sofia tilted her head and blinked at him. Sara looked like she was trying not to throw up.

"We're going to miss having you around," Mr. Crickett said to me. He cleared his throat. For a second his face got as splotchy as Raymond's tended to do. He turned to Raymond. "It's nice having a friend, isn't it, son?"

Sofia squeezed Mr. Crickett's arm.

"The thing is," I said, "there are a few things I need to do in Wayward."

Mr. Crickett raised an eyebrow at me. "Well, I guess you best be taking that agenda up with your dad. You hitched a ride to this wagon, and I'm the one directing its path."

He stared steadily at me. I knew that look; it was the same one Daddy gave me when there would be no considering of options.

"What are the chances your dad will be there right on time?" Raymond asked.

I put my head on my knees and moaned. We were in the backseat of the truck. According to Mr. Crickett's map on his phone, which he had attached to the dashboard, we'd be at the Wayward Bluegrass Festival at 11:55.

Mr. Crickett's phone buzzed with an incoming message, which the phone read aloud. *"This is Ernie. I'll be there a couple of minutes before noon. Let Trixy know, okay?"*

I heard the message in Dad's voice despite the computer being the one doing the speaking, and I didn't think it was because of Gran's magic. It was because I missed him, and because I wanted him to give me a great big hug, and because I wanted to go home.

But mostly it was because I was going to break his heart. Again.

"When we get there," I whispered to Raymond, "I'm going to need you to distract our dads."

"Oh, no, Trixy." He shook his head so fast his cheeks turned to quivering Jell-O. "I don't like the way you're scheming again."

"I'm so close, Raymond! I need to hear the rest of Dollie's story."

His face scrunched. "Oh, stars, Trixy. Not again with the running away!"

"When we get there, I'm going to need to figure out where Aunt Elise lived. Or Henry's farm! I bet loads of folks know the Michaelson Canning Factory, so I should be able to find something. We're so close! I can't stop now."

With all of Daddy's "start fresh" talk, I knew if I didn't uncover Gran's story now, I likely never would.

Mr. Crickett pulled the truck to a dusty stop following the direction of a teenager wearing a fluorescent green vest and waving a red baton. Mr. Crickett had rolled down the window and told the boy that he was one of the performers and should have a reserved spot near the front. The boy shook his head and pointed to the spot in front of him with the baton. "Park here," he said. Mr. Crickett did. Funny how almost no one listens to teenagers, but put one in a fluorescent vest and give him a baton, and everyone falls in line.

Mr. Crickett pulled his phone off the dash. "I'll text your dad that we'll meet at the ticket stand."

"Okay," I said, careful not to look at Raymond. "I'm just going to run to the bathroom first. Meet you there!" With that, I darted between parked cars in the general direction of the carnival.

"She must really have to go," Mr. Crickett said.

"Yeah, me too," Raymond said.

"Hold on!" Mr. Crickett said.

Sara turned as Raymond sprinted after me, her eyebrows peaked. "Oh, come on, Dad! You saw how much cocoa they were drinking at the diner. The last thing you want is one of them having an accident."

If I made it out of this scheming, I was going to give Sara Crickett a giant hug. Raymond Crickett? Not so much! He was supposed to distract our dads, not follow me!

A few seconds later, Raymond huffed and puffed as he crouched behind a minivan next to me. I glared at him.

"I made a promise," he whispered, "and I'm going to keep it."

"What promise?" I snapped.

Raymond glared right back at me. "When Gran died, your mama asked me to be your friend, even when you didn't deserve it, for at least one year."

"She did *what*?"

Raymond nodded. "She said you'd both be needing someone, and she might not always be able to be that someone for you." He leaned closer to me. "Let me tell you, Trixy, it ain't been an easy promise to keep."

My mouth couldn't form words as too many thoughts flew toward it. Raymond shushed me. "There they are!" He pointed to the ticket stand where Mr. Crickett stood with his back toward us. In front of him was Daddy. He looked the same as ever, big and broad and a little annoyed. A lot annoyed, to tell you the truth.

I tugged on Raymond's sleeve and, still crouched, we backed from behind the van and then darted right by our dads, under a rope gate, and into the festival without them ever seeing us. "Oh, no," Raymond said a moment later, as throngs of people passed us on both sides. "We didn't get tickets! We could get in trouble for sneaking in."

I put a hand on each of Raymond's shoulders. "I don't know if you realize this, but we're already in big trouble. Best we can do is make the most of it."

Raymond looked around. "I'm guessing you don't mean by getting waffles and ice cream."

I dropped my arms. "No, we've got to find someone old enough to tell us about the Michaelson Canning Factory. Maybe where Henry lived."

He sighed. "All right. Let's go find some old people."

Finding old people was easy at the bluegrass festival.

They all were sitting in a curve in front of the stage, shifting their legs so they didn't stick to the vinyl lawn chairs they'd brought in. Most fanned themselves with paper programs or clipped little battery-operated fans to their chair arms. On stage, three people in flannel and overalls plucked or drew their bows across strings in a bluegrass cover of a rock song about wayward sons. The women clapped along to the beat and the men tapped their feet.

My stomach felt like soup, simmering, simmering, simmering, about to boil. Daddy was here. He and Mr. Crickett were looking for us. The soup was a bubbly mess of guilt, anxiety, and hope. Because the rest of Gran's story was here too. I *felt* it.

All around the festival was buzzing, plucking, crooning, eating, laughing, cheering—it was all too much. My ears vibrated. I pressed my hands against them, but the sound wasn't muffled. I realized this was something else, something new. Like all around me, people's untold stories were tumbling over one another. There was something *here*, something *close*, that Gran needed me to hear.

"How do we do this?" Raymond asked. "Should we look for someone with a Michaelson Canning Factory T-shirt or something?"

"Don't be ridiculous, Raymond," I snapped. *As though people wore canning factory T-shirts!*

An old man wearing what looked like an even older black cowboy hat shuffled forward with a banjo slung around his back. As he walked, people rose from their lawn chairs to shake his hand or pat his back. "How's your family?" one man asked. "Haven't seen y'all in church lately."

"Fine, fine," the man said. His voice was smooth and sweet. "The ole missus will be here for part of the show."

He tugged on a beard that looked just like Mr. Crickett's, except his was pure white.

The buzzing in my ears flared, then paused as he continued by us.

The man's brown T-shirt had *Michaelson's* in fancy script across the top and a big white can of peas printed on it.

Raymond had the nerve to grin at me, his mouth stretching back with smugness.

Chapter Twenty-Four

The old man headed to the side of the stage. Though we called out, "Sir! Sir!" the man continued on. He pulled back a tarp hanging along the side of the stage and let it drop behind him.

We paused just outside it. Would it be okay to follow him inside or would we be walking ourselves into further trouble? "Maybe there's someone else. . . ." Raymond whispered.

Just then a man wearing a big white badge on his buttoned-down shirt half ran, half walked toward the stage. The performers were exiting the far side as an announcer was heading across. The man with the badge motioned to the announcer, gesturing for him to bend over and hear him. Raymond and I ducked down.

The man with the badge had to hold his knees and suck air before speaking. "Kids," he gasped. "Runaways. Here. Their dads. Looking. For them."

The announcer held the microphone behind him. "There are runaway kids here?"

The badge man nodded, and then straightened. "Yes. A girl and a boy. Ten years old, both of them. One—the girl—has run away before. Their parents are wild with worry, man. Wild. One of the dads is in the headlining band! Won't go onstage without knowing where his kid is. See if you can stall a little."

The announcer sighed. "Kids today!" He nodded and waved the man with the badge away.

"Oh, no," Raymond said. "Oh, no. Oh, no. Oh, no!" His face skipped the red splotches and went straight to a shade of pickle.

"Pull it together, Raymond," I said. "Maybe the guy got the details wrong. I mean, how worried could our dads be? We've only been gone a few minutes." I peered across the festival. Police officers or security officers seemed to be weaving through every row, many of them with their hands cupped over walkie-talkies. I put my arm out the way Mama did whenever she had to suddenly brake the car, holding Raymond in place. "Okay, so new plan. Let's be real quick and find that old man."

Raymond and I ducked behind the tarp.

When Gran first told me about the beehive in Henry's barn, I pictured all of those bees tumbling over one another, every one of them hustling as they did their job to keep the hive running. What we saw behind the tarp was a lot like that, only musicians with banjos, fiddles, and guitars. Somewhere among them, Mr. Crickett's band probably was warming up.

We kept our heads low. Raymond's chest heaved. "I've never been a criminal, Trixy."

"You're not a *criminal*, Raymond. Running away isn't a crime." I scratched behind my ear. "I mean, I don't *think* so. It shouldn't be, anyways."

"Your mama told me to be your friend. She told me I was a good influence on you. But you know what? *You* are a *bad* influence on me!"

I elbowed him in the ribs. "Pull it together, Raymond! Think of this as, I don't know, an adventure."

Someone chuckled behind us. *The old man!* "Be cautious 'round a woman who promises you adventure, son." He lowered himself onto a crate beside the stage and winked at Raymond, who stood there with his mouth hanging open.

A huge black horsefly swooped near poor Raymond. I swatted it away, and Raymond flinched as though I would slap him. “You have trust issues,” I told him.

“Oh, you *think*, Trixy?”

“Trixy,” the old man repeated. “Now, where did I hear that name?”

“From the policemen looking for us, most likely,” Raymond blurted.

I elbowed him again. “There’s a time and a place for the truth.”

“Beliefs such as those are what got us into this life of crime!” Raymond hissed.

The old man chuckled, then held out his hand to shake. “Folks ’round here call me Hank Sting. Now what are two jailbirds like you doing in Wayward?”

I pointed to his T-shirt. “We’re looking for the Michaelson Canning Factory. Or anyone who might know anything about it.”

“I know a thing or two,” the old man said.

“Did you work there?” I asked.

He nodded. “Matter of fact, I did, but that was a long time ago.”

The trio of women playing on stage stopped to loud applause. The announcer called over the microphone: “Please be on the lookout for two children who need to be reunited with their parents. If you see a small girl with dark hair and brown eyes, and a boy with blondish hair, likely being dragged around by her, contact a security official right away."

Hank Sting raised a furry eyebrow. Raymond took a deep breath. "Please, we're in a hurry. The Michaelson family farm, do you know where it is?"

"It'd have a big red barn outside," I cut in. "The barn is—or was—full of bees, right inside the wall. Do you know it?"

Mr. Sting stood. He looked from the stage, to us, and then down to his feet. "I don't know what's going on here or how much I want to be involved."

"Please," I said, feeling like Daddy trying to talk on blasting days. The buzzing in my ears was so loud I couldn't even hear my own words until they left my mouth. "I need to know—do you know where it is? Or where I could find the Michaelsons? Maybe you know a Henry Michaelson? He knew my gran; that's why I'm here. She lived with her aunt for a while, Elise Jacobs. Do you know them?"

The old man looked up. "I haven't heard Elise's name in a long time."

"You knew her?" I grabbed his arm and he stared hard at my face. Maybe he heard the buzzing too. For a moment, the sound shifted to the whisper of a little boy, too high pitched for me to make out the words.

The announcer strode in our direction. Raymond and I darted to the side of the stage, crouching in the shadow of it, and Mr. Sting stepped in front us, blocking us further. "Hank," the announcer said, "Crickett Quintet is next to go, but the lead player's son is one of those missing kids. We gotta stall or a lot of folks here are gonna make a ruckus. Those boys are our main draw! You up for it?"

The announcer disappeared back on stage, taking it for granted that Hank was in.

"Oh, no," Raymond moaned. He grabbed fistfuls of his hair. "If he doesn't perform, he won't get paid! Then the rest of the tour is over. He's going to be so mad at me, Trixy! I can't do this to him."

I nodded. We were so close, but he was right. "I know," I whispered.

Hank Sting didn't look at us as he rocked on his heels. He rubbed on his chest with his knuckles. "Give me a minute," he muttered. Then he swung the banjo around from behind him and pulled in a big breath. The honey of his voice turned sharp. "I'll help you," he said. "I knew Aunt Elise. I knew your gran."

His next words fell into the curve of my ear, sounding as though spoken by a little boy. "Hank Sting is my stage name. I'm Henry Michaelson." He looked at me, and though he didn't speak, I heard it anyway, in the voice of a little boy. *Worth the sting.*

"I'll help you," he said. "I'll tell you whatever you want to know. But you have to help me first." The corner of the tarp was yanked back, and two security officers stepped inside. Hank—*Henry*—tipped his hat toward them and sidestepped so we were still in the shadow. Turning to us, he whispered. "I've got a plan to help us all."

Hank (*Henry!*) strolled up onto the stage, holding the banjo lightly in his hands. The announcer said, "Well, lookie here! It's Wayward's own, Hank Sting! What a treat to have the legendary musician perform for us today. Hank was the 1967 winner of this here festival. Can you believe it?"

Raymond and I stood on tiptoe to look out across the stage onto the field. Most of the people watching the festival were on their feet, clapping for Henry. He nodded at them and hoisted his banjo to applause. The buzzing finally dampened in my ears.

He adjusted the strap of the banjo and then stood with one leg on a little stool, letting the banjo rest against it. For a moment, he didn't say anything, just looked down on it like he was listening. The security guards continued to weave through the crowd. I spotted Sara's vibrant blue hair. She was walking beside the stage, her cane sweeping in front of her. Mr. Crickett was a few feet from her, scanning the crowd. Daddy was on the other side of the field, peeking through the tents and trailers where vendors were selling food. The sun was high in a baby-blue sky.

A man, a little older than Mama, held the arm of an old woman, guiding her to a seat smack dab in the middle of the first row. As though he had heard them, Henry looked up and tipped his faded cowboy hat at them. Gently, he strummed the strings.

"This one's going to take me back a ways," he said into the microphone. For a moment, it felt like everyone there inhaled at the same time, his voice quieting them all. He let go of the strings and rubbed his knuckles against the middle of his chest. "And it's going to sting a bit," he added softer. "But I have a hunch it'll be worth it."

The strumming deepened and Henry straightened. My mind whirled. He had done it—somehow Henry had grown up to be a musician. I'd bet anything the faded black hat on his head was the same one Dollie and Lil Sis had given him that summer.

Henry glanced over his shoulder at us. In that moment, I heard a little boy's voice, clear as though he whispered right into my ears. *She was my age, and she was glamorous. A movie star. Nothing seemed to scare her.* On and on the story went, faster than I would've been able to hear in actual words—a story about a girl who would change his life. About a girl he risked everything to impress. A girl who had been sent away because of him. A girl who made sure her sister could come back. He told me how he and Lil Sis wished for her on a star every night for years. *A girl who came back.*

Had she come back to Henry? To Lil Sis?

This story ends sad. I didn't hear that in Henry's child voice. I heard it in Raymond's. That was what he had warned. Was it true?

Henry began to hum a familiar melody.

"*Trixy,*" Raymond said. In front of us, the tarp bent back. We pressed against the shadows as a flash of blue moved near us. Raymond whimpered.

On stage, Henry said, "Now, I hear there are two kids making a ruckus at this here festival. I was a kid once, not so long ago, and I sure remember getting into heaps of trouble. Weren't ever my idea, I assure you, but my fault all the same." To this, the audience whistled and hooted.

The tarp flipped open again. A security guard came through, walkie-talkie to his mouth. At the same time, something rustled behind us. Raymond gripped my arm and we peeked over our shoulders. It was Daddy. Mr. Crick-ett just behind him. "Trixy?" Daddy called, hands cupped around his mouth. Mr. Crickett shouted Raymond's name.

"We're in so much trouble," Raymond whined.

Up on stage, Henry leaned into the microphone. "How 'bout we help those kids out? Trixy, Raymond, c'mon up here on stage. Let's show your folks you're fine, and maybe delay them laying into you for a spell."

Raymond gripped my arm. "That old man is going to get us killed!" he said at the same time I said, "That old man's a genius!"

"Think about it," I told Raymond. "If we're there, our dads know we're okay. They have a minute to calm down. Then your dad goes on stage and performs, and Henry and I walk off to talk to *my* dad. Genius!"

Raymond's eyes narrowed as he listened to me, then suddenly bugged. His mouth dropped open.

I shuddered. "My dad's right behind me, isn't he?"

Right on cue, someone grabbed my shoulder, whipping me around, and I was face to face with Daddy, looking angrier than a bee confronted with black socks.

Chapter Twenty-Five

Here's the jagged-edge story that ripped Gran apart, piece by piece, the one I promised never to tell. The one that made her disappear into her bedroom with the door pressed shut every year on February third. The story she fought so hard to keep inside, despite it clawing her apart.

This is the story she shared only once and only with me.

Every February third, I would ask Mama why Gran wouldn't come out of her bedroom, why I could hear her crying in there. Mama would shake her head and turn up the radio to muffle those sobs. Mama's jaw would set. "Something happened to her on this day, not that she ever would tell me what. I've long since stopped asking her to explain. Just let it go, Trixy. She'll be back to herself tomorrow."

And every year, that's what I would do. Except the day I didn't.

On that day, I pretended to go to Raymond's house, but really I looped around to the outside of Gran's bedroom window. I upturned a bucket from the shed and stood on it to peer into the room. Standing like that made me wobbly, so I hugged the window frame instead and pressed my ear against the cool glass.

There I was, my ear pressed flat against the glass, when Gran suddenly jerked the window up, sending my arms windmilling and my body tilting backward. She grabbed me by my shoulders, pinning my arms to my sides, and lifted me straight into the room. Before my feet touched the ground, she squeezed me to her.

And she told me about loneliness.

About leaving childhood behind and running, not away, but toward something new—toward being on her own instead of one half of a whole. She told me about seeing the snowy mountains in Montana, the shadow of ancient trees in California, the sunset over a desert in Nevada, the moss growing over treetops in New Orleans, how in each of these places, she had been trying to find a place she had fit, like a puzzle piece left in the box.

How one day, still not knowing where she belonged, she realized a baby had begun to grow in her belly.

"How could I take care of a baby when I didn't yet know how to take care of myself?" she asked, but I knew she wasn't asking me. Her eyes didn't even meet mine. I think she might've been asking the world, and it scared me.

She told me about switching from trying to find a place for herself to going back to where she had come from to secure a home for the baby. A place with people who loved each other, people who had figured out how to be whole. She told me about the baby's eyes, how they were as blue as the sky and just as wondrous. She told me her arms have felt empty ever since that day, but she knew her baby's heart never would be. She told me she left him and never looked back, would never go back. And then she told me that, years later, when she again had a chance to be a mother, she still didn't feel whole, but she managed to be enough.

"Mama has a brother?" I blurted, my heart hammering.

"Hush, Trixy! Hush!" Gran gasped, her hands rushing to her mouth as though sweeping the story back inside.

When she couldn't, Gran seemed to be made of pebbles that toppled all around me. *Don't tell her*, Gran begged me. *Don't ever speak of it! Please, let me be the one to tell her. In the right way, at the right time!*

And so I promised I'd unhear the story.

I meant to keep that promise, Gran. Truly, I did.

Chapter Twenty-Six

I played one last nasty trick on my dad, something I hadn't done since I was four years old and better practiced at misbehaving.

The Wet Noodle.

All my limbs turned to overboiled pasta, slipping through his grasp. Then I sprinted up those stage stairs.

Henry's banjo gained speed as I darted forward. For a moment, I was frozen in place by applause, but then a soft hand slipped into mine. Raymond, beside me.

"This is going to be one heck of a sting," he muttered.

Together, we walked across the stage to where Henry stood, a huge smile on his face. Once there, he took off his hat, revealing a swirl of gray-white hair. He popped the hat on my head. "I'm going to wager you might've heard this song before," he said, and began to play about wishing on a star. I squeezed Raymond's hand.

For the first time, I let myself believe this was real.

Henry really was in front of me, singing this song because he knew it meant so much to Gran. And Gran meant so much to him.

Her stories were real. They were true. And they still mattered.

Something stirred on the side of the stage. Dad. Mr. Crickett was beside him, both standing on the edge of the stage now. The announcer stepped out then, his hands up, blocking them. They seemed to be whisper-yelling back and forth.

Henry winked and handed me the microphone. With a shaking voice, I started singing. I'm good at a lot of things, but singing isn't one of them. I pushed the microphone toward Raymond.

"C'mon," I whispered, dropping his hand. "Help a girl out!"

"Helping you out is what got us into this mess," Raymond hissed back.

The microphone picked up all of that, and soon the audience was laughing so hard I forgot to be annoyed with Raymond or nervous about performing or scared of being in trouble. Raymond took a deep breath and started to sing. But three words in, he faltered. "I forget the words. I only really sing with family," he told the audience. The whisper-shouting on the side of the stage was getting louder. "Oh, man, we're in trouble, Trix!"

I turned toward clicking steps from the far side of the stage. Sara, her blue hair shining in the lights and sunglasses on her face, headed toward us. "I got you," she said. She put her hand on Raymond's shoulder and began to sing with him.

The audience hushed as Raymond's and Sara's voices intertwined. *There's magic in stars.* And in sisters.

I stepped aside as the Crickett Quintet—minus Mr. Crickett—joined us. The crowd cheered, some people going to their feet. The song morphed into the one about the wonderful world, Sara's clear voice rolling out over the crowd as Raymond stepped to the side, giving her the spotlight. And then the announcer put down his stop sign arms so Mr. Crickett could stride toward his children. One of the band members kicked his fiddle case to slide toward him, and Mr. Crickett unsnapped it and raised it to his shoulder.

Sara grinned as Mr. Crickett played over Raymond's head. Raymond sang the melody lower than Sara's bold, strong voice. The three of them stood a little away from the band, Henry, and me. They seemed to be their own entity, their own world.

I thought about the story I swore I'd never tell, about what it meant to be true, to be real, to be whole.

Henry tapped my shoulder and motioned for me to follow him to the side of the stage. Daddy was waiting for me there, and though Mr. Crickett seemed to have put aside his anger, something told me Daddy would be just as mad now as the moment I had wet-noodled him.

I let Henry take the lead. Daddy waited for us, alternatively shoving his hands in his back pockets and crossing his arms. When I got closer to him, I forgot that I was in major trouble and rushed ahead, throwing my arms around his waist. Daddy knelt and squeezed me back. "I'm sorry," I said into his chest.

He took a deep breath. "I know."

"I love you," I told him.

"Love you back." I looked at him then. Daddy's jaw was set but his face softened a little with a tight smile. "We've got an eight-hour drive home. Plenty of time for the three of us to talk this through."

"Three?" My face scrunched. *Was Raymond coming back with us?*

"*That,*" Daddy said with a sigh, "is what I've been wanting to tell you." He stepped aside, and there, standing a few feet away, was Mama. Her thin hands held a pile of stories, all of them mine. All of them Dollie's. Her eyes darted back and forth across my face as though reading a map. The air was trapped inside my lungs and my heart stopped hammering with a sudden thud.

"I've been working hard on getting better," Mom said. "But it took a lot of convincing for my therapist to agree to give me a pass for the day, and I need to get back to treatment as soon as possible." She lifted the stack of stories I had left behind. "I've read all of these stories, Trixy."

How can feelings be so mushed together? How can one person feel so much all at once? I couldn't sort through any of them. I was angry—still so angry with her, though I didn't know why—and brokenhearted and happy and, oh, stars, how I missed my mama.

She smiled. "It's okay. Whatever you're feeling, it's—" I ran to her, squeezing her so close, making sure she was real, making sure she hadn't disappeared.

"My," Henry said, and cleared his throat as Daddy's shoulders quaked beside him. "There's a lot happening here, huh?" He glanced behind him toward the barrier between backstage and the field. "How would you folks like to join my family for supper tonight? I think we might all benefit from a sit-down."

Daddy held out his hand to shake Henry's. "That's kind

of you, sir, but we'll grab dinner on the way. We've intruded enough."

"We can't go!" I said, and then flinched a bit at Daddy's expression.

Mama peppered the top of my head with kisses. "At the very least, we need to wait until the Cricketts are off stage. I'd like to thank them."

Daddy narrowed his eyes at me, but Henry cut in before he could reply. "Well, that's just fine because I'm going to have to insist that you meet my wife." He put his hand on Daddy's shoulder and nodded toward Mama. "You're going to want to meet her." Something in the old man's face must've affected them, because they exchanged a glance.

"Your wife?" I repeated.

The tarp behind us lifted and a man with striking blue eyes stepped through, holding the edge for an old woman. A man with eyes as blue as the sky. And beside him, my gran.

I stumbled backward, my voice stoppered in my throat. I saw that same face, her hand patting my leg. I saw flashing lights and a terrible crash.

Mama caught me. Her arm curled around my shoulder, holding me up and holding herself together all at once. I whimpered and forced myself to really look.

The woman wasn't Gran.

But she looked so much like Gran that Daddy said her name at the same time Mama gasped and I felt the ground spin around me. “This is my wife,” Henry said. “Her name’s Dorothy. But most folks call her Dollie.”

“No,” I said, only it came out as a yelp. “No, that can’t be Dollie. Dollie was my gran and she’s gone.”

I sucked in my breath. *Gone.* But was she? The old woman flinched as though I had slapped her.

No, my brain insisted again. *Dollie was Gran. If this woman was Dollie, that meant my gran was . . .*

Henry knelt in front of me. “Dolcie, your gran, was *Lil Sis.* Dorothy, my wife, is *Dollie,*” he whispered. His voice louder, he said, “Here’s the thing, Trixy Mae Jacobs Williams. We know you. Lil Sis kept us in the loop. We know all about you and”—here he glanced at Mama—“your family and your gran, though I never dreamed I’d see y’all in front of me.” He stepped aside, and Dorothy—*Dollie*—stepped forward.

“Trixy?” she whispered. “Is it really you?”

I stared at her, all of my words turning to dandelion seeds, flying away with every breath I managed. She was taller than Gran, her nose narrower and chin pointier. Her wrinkles deeper. Her hair was long, flowing down her back thick and straight. Her voice, though. Her voice was the same as Gran’s. A voice that settled in my ears and soothed all the bees inside. I braced myself for any of her untold stories, but I didn't hear one.

Daddy stepped forward. "I'm not sure what's going on here." He looked from Henry to Dollie and then to the younger man standing just beside them. "But my wife hasn't been well and—"

All my words, all my thoughts, everything slammed back into me at last. "No!" I burst out. "*No.* My gran, *she* was Dollie. She lost Lil Sis. She never saw her anymore! This isn't right."

The old woman shuddered, tears flowing down her cheeks. The man beside her looped his arm around her waist. She leaned into him a moment. "I suspected. When she didn't write for weeks, I suspected. If I'm being honest, I knew sooner than that. But hearing you say *was* all the same, it hurts. She's gone, isn't she?"

When someone dies, it doesn't happen just once.

Gran died over and over again, every time I woke in the morning after my dreams let me forget.

She died again when Raymond's eyes met mine on my first day back to school.

When Gran's dentist called to schedule a cleaning.

When the other grandmas at the park stretched on tiptoe to see if she was with me.

Whenever I saw the lilacs blooming over her grave.

Every time she died, it hurt.

Henry led us to a half circle of crates backstage. We sat facing one another, and, after a while, the puzzle pieces pushed together.

I told Dollie (*How could it be Dollie?*) that Gran had whispered stories about them all my life. "But I always thought she was Dollie, because Dollie was the hero of all the stories."

The real Dollie laughed. "We each did everything we could to make the other the star," she said. Her laugh was like Gran's too. Somehow it both hurt and soothed to hear it. I wanted to crawl onto her lap and feel her push my hair behind my ear the way Gran always had. But I curled into Mama instead.

Mama gave her my pile of stories, and Dollie and Henry looked through them, reading snippets aloud. Next to them, seemingly as astonished as Mama and Daddy, was the now-grown baby that Gran had found a different home for, my uncle Steve.

I have an uncle. The thought was a loop playing again and again in my mind. Next to me, Mama's eyes were wide as she watched the man. *I have a brother*, I saw playing on repeat in her mind, as well. "I can't believe she never told me," Mama whispered. "I missed out on so much of her life."

Dollie patted Mama's leg. "She thought she was doing the best thing for you by giving you a life separate from all these stories that haunted her." She shuffled the pages on her lap. "But she couldn't escape them."

Dollie told us that Lil Sis had brought the baby to them a few years after she and Henry had gotten married. She left the baby and promised to never come back, promised to put herself together without complicating their lives. "But we wanted her to be there," Dollie said. "We couldn't convince her of that, but we made sure he always knew she loved him, just that her love was . . ."

"Complicated," Mama said sadly. "There is so much I didn't know. Don't know."

Dollie nodded. "We're all broken pieces, aren't we? Only for some of us, the glue that holds us together is tougher. Lil Sis? Hers was stretched pretty thin. I think there were gaps that she tried desperately to ignore."

Mama took a deep breath. "So much of what I thought was true—"

I leaned into her side. "It was mostly true, almost real." Some of the pieces that made me, the memories of Gran and me, were shifting inside. Maybe cracking a little bit here and there as they made room for these stories she had left untold. Gran wasn't perfect, not like I had remembered. She hadn't always been the hero of her stories. But that glue that Dollie talked about? That was made up of how much Gran loved me, and it wasn't ever going to stop holding me together.

Chapter Twenty-Seven

Once upon a time, two sisters who raised each other were sent in different directions.

After leaving the Society for Friendless Children, Dollie and Lil Sis wrote letters. Lil Sis told her about Henry singing at the county fair. About wearing a flouncy dress to prom with Henry. About helping Aunt Elise in the garden. About Henry having dinner at their table.

Dollie didn't share anything about her years with Mother, except to write they were harder than they might have been. She mailed her sister a little square of paper. *Worth the sting.*

On her eighteenth birthday, Dollie came back to Wayward. She found a job at a bakery in town and moved into an apartment above it. Lil Sis asked to move in with her, but Dollie insisted she finish high school with Aunt Elise. And though something twisted deep and painfully in her heart at the way Lil Sis looked at Henry, she stayed away from him too.

Only she couldn't keep Henry from the bakery. And he came to the shop every morning and night to have Dollie's specialty, a danish filled with sweet cream.

One day, Lil Sis finally saw the way Henry looked at Dollie, and something shattered inside her. She realized all she had and all that she was, down to her name, was because of her sister. She realized all that her sister did, she did for her. And she knew that her sister would never let herself love Henry so long as she also loved him.

And so Lil Sis left, breaking her sister's heart, to make each of them whole.

Dollie sighed as she sat in front of us on the crate. By now, the festival was nearly over. The Crickett Quintet had left the stage to thunderous applause.

Raymond and Sara sat with us, laughing as we shared stories about Dollie and Lil Sis.

When someone dies, it happens over and over.

When someone shares a story, they live over and over.

After Dollie told us about Lil Sis moving from Wayward, we all were quiet for a moment.

"Lil Sis . . . Dolcie didn't give us any way to reach her. She'd send us post cards, though." She patted Steve's hand. "When she finally did return, it was because Steve was on his way."

"February third," Mama whispered. "That's your birthday, isn't it?"

Uncle Steve nodded. I finally shared the story I had tried so hard to keep quiet, letting it rustle to the surface. I told them how Gran had cried every February third, and how she finally told me why. How she carried him in her heart. Telling them the hush-hush story felt like shaking off a heavy sweater in the middle of August. Afterward, for just a moment, my ears tingled. Uncle Steve's eyes closed. When he opened them, Mama smiled back at him.

"It's going to take some getting used to, but I'm happy to have a big brother," Mama said. She laughed, and I realized I had been wrong—Dollie's laugh wasn't just like Gran's. It was like Mama's.

Steve—*Uncle* Steve—told us he was married. That he had three kids, and one of them was a girl my age. I had cousins! Mama pressed her hands against her mouth. "I'm an aunt," she whispered.

"You know," Dollie said to Mama, "when she left Steve with us, she swore she'd never return. We begged her to stay, but she wanted him to have a home, and she didn't think she was capable of creating one as strong as the one Henry and I could provide. She said it was better for our lives to follow separate paths. We worried we'd never hear from her again. But she started writing to us when she was expecting you."

Dollie turned to me. "She told us everything about you, Trixy. She told us you were a storyteller and a story*keeper*. And that she was going to tell you the truth, best she could manage, so that one day, when she was brave enough, you'd know why she wanted to come here. She said you'd hear all of our stories, and she made sure we heard yours."

Dollie invited us back to stay the night on the farm, but Daddy said we needed to go home since Mama had an appointment in the morning and I was grounded.

I had kind of hoped he had forgotten about the running away business.

"Ah, go easy on the kid," Mr. Crickett told Daddy. "Maybe it wasn't right for Trixy to leave the way she did, but I sure am glad she was with us." He smiled at Raymond and Sara. Sara made her internally-rolling-eyes snort and Raymond blushed. As they waved good-bye and turned to leave, I clobbered Raymond with a hug.

"You're my best friend, Raymond Crickett," I told him.

Raymond didn't hug me back. "When I get back home,"

he said, "we're going to have to talk about how you ought to treat your friends, Trixy. Lying to them, getting them in big trouble, being mean more than you're not, that's not how someone treats a friend."

"I know," I said. "And I'm sorry."

Raymond pushed me back a little, but not in a mean way. More like he needed to breathe. "So, what are you going to tell Catrina?" he asked. "About the contest, I mean."

"Catrina? I forgot all about her," I said. "I haven't decided yet." But that was a lie. I was going to enter that contest, and I was going to win.

We made plans to come back to Wayward in a few months, once Mama had plenty of time to work with the outpatient program. We'd see the farm. "We still have some bees," Henry told me, tweaking my nose. "But I'm a lot better at getting to the honey now."

I took off his hat and held it out to him. Henry laughed and put it back on my head. "Keep it," he said. "It looks better on you."

"There is so much I want to know about Lil Sis," Dollie said to Mama, her hand over her heart. "Was she happy? Her letters sounded happy, but I don't know if that's the truth."

"The truth is," Mama told her, "she loved us. She loved

us as honestly and real as she could. And I believe she loves us still."

Mama, Daddy, and I held hands as we walked to our truck that night.

The brightest star in the sky twinkled at me. *I love you,* I told it. *Thank you for loving me. I'll miss you forever.*

Acknowledgments

Much love to Reka Simonsen, whose vision and mindful edits elevated this book to new heights. What a joy it has been to work with you! Thank you also to superagent Nicole Resciniti, for falling for Trixy's story and making sure it was heard.

Thank you to everyone at Atheneum who has had a hand in creating this book, including copy editor Ellen Winkler, managing editor Clare McGlade, and jacket designer Debra Sfetsios-Conover. Thank you, Oriol Vidal, for the stunning cover illustration.

I was lucky be raised among powerful storytellers who made everyday moments seem magical. These include my mom and dad, Valetta and Steve Baumgardner, and my grandparents, Harold and Lois Baumgardner. My papaw passed as this book was being written, but his stories stay with us. While some of his recollections might not be true ("I guess I'm afraid that I won't get rich while I'm still young enough to enjoy it. So to deal with it, I just spend what I have as fast I get it."), they're all real. His journal entry on losing his own grandparent lives in my heart. "It's not so bad. It's just like going into the next room. And it will only be a short time till we're together again."

In writing this book, I reimagined many stories that, stitched together, create the fabric of my life. I'm grateful for those who helped iron out the details. This includes beekeeper Mary Nisi, who shared the difference between swarming and attacks, and told me why beekeeper suits are never black. Much appreciation and gratitude to Jen Petro-Roy, whose expert read and insight helped ensure that this book's depiction of an eating disorder was accurate without being harmful. Lots of love to Kari Adams and Kirsten Shaw for helping me hash out Raymond's diner scene; to Trixy Bemis for the name inspiration; and to Jon, Emma, and Ben for the cross-Tennessee road trip. Twice.

More thanks to my daughter, Emma, for helping me be sure Sara's depiction of life as a person with low vision is authentic. Much appreciation to my son, Ben, who helped problem solve plot points during our quarantine hikes. And so much love to Jon for making coffee every morning and for always being in my corner.